"Why are you so mad?" Shana asked him.

He hesitated a few seconds. "I'm not. I'm tired."

"You've become increasingly irritated for two weeks."

"And you've become increasingly calm."

It sounded like an accusation. "That's a bad thing?" When Kincaid didn't answer, she said, "Would you prefer I go back to my own bed?" She could hardly form the words, but she didn't know what else to do.

"No," he said, his voice harsh.

"Do you...want me to leave?" She swallowed around the hot lump in her throat.

He finally looked directly at her. "No."

"Then what *do* you want?"

Dear Reader,

It's been said that you can't go home again. For Shana Callahan that's a good thing. Home was difficult, so difficult that she ran away and stayed away for ten years. Now she's back in her small hometown of Chance City, all grown up and wanting to make amends. She's trying to prove she's changed and has been walking a gossip-free path for a year now. She *is* home, but it's a new kind of home.

Landon Kincaid wants to help the struggling, pride-filled single mother. The way he goes about it, however, puts her squarely back in the gossip zone. But sometimes emotion trumps reputation, and success trumps pride. And sometimes love is all that matters.

I hope you enjoy Shana and Kincaid's journey as much I enjoyed sending them on it.

Susan Crosby

ALMOST A CHRISTMAS BRIDE

SUSAN CROSBY

SPECIAL EDITION

Recycling programs
for this product may
not exist in your area.

ISBN-13: 978-0-373-65639-4

ALMOST A CHRISTMAS BRIDE

Copyright © 2011 by Susan Bova Crosby

This edition published by arrangement with Harlequin Books S.A.

For questions and comments about the quality of this book please contact us
at Customer_eCare@Harlequin.ca.

® and TM are trademarks of Harlequin Books S.A., used under license.
Trademarks indicated with ® are registered in the United States Patent
and Trademark Office, the Canadian Trade Marks Office and in other
countries.

www.Harlequin.com

Printed in U.S.A.

Other titles by Susan Crosby available in ebook

SUSAN CROSBY

believes in the value of setting goals, but also in the magic of making wishes, which often do come true—as long as she works hard enough. Along life's journey, she's done a lot of the usual things—married, had children, attended college a little later than the average coed and earned a B.A. in English. Then she dove off the deep end into a full-time writing career, a wish come true.

Susan enjoys writing about people who take a chance on love, sometimes against all odds. She loves warm, strong heroes and good-hearted, self-reliant heroines, and she will always believe in happily-ever-after.

More can be learned about her at www.susancrosby.com.

For Lori and Justin.
You're proof that the institution of marriage thrives
in these modern times. I'm so proud of both of you.

Chapter One

Shana Callahan had learned long ago not to get her hopes up, but this morning butterflies of anticipation were flitting in her stomach. She pressed a hand against her abdomen as she punched the elevator button for the third floor of the downtown Sacramento office building. The elevator seemed to climb in slow motion as her employer's words echoed in her head again and again. "The job would be long-term, Shana. And it's in Chance City."

Chance City, the place where'd she grown up, run away from at eighteen and then finally come back to after ten years away. *Home.*

No more hour-long commute to Sacramento for whatever temp job she'd been placed in that day or week. No more crossing her fingers that her car would survive the trip. No more worrying about rain or fog or accidents adding extra time to her commute. If it took ten minutes to get across town in Chance City, it was because someone hailed you down to talk.

She tried to imagine anyone from her small town contacting an employment agency instead of just tacking an ad to the bulletin board at the local diner, where most transactions were made, but no one came to mind.

The elevator door opened. Shana followed the hallway to the office of At Your Service, a high-end clerical-and-domestic-help temp agency often nicknamed "Wives for Hire" by clients, and owned by the elegant, unflappable Julia Swanson.

"Hey, Shana," the receptionist, Missy, called out. "Julia said to send you straight back. She'll be there in a second."

Julia's office was as soothing as the woman herself, the color palette muted, the furniture classic. On the wall behind her tidy mahogany desk hung the company logo, with "When you need the personal touch…" in gold lettering below it. It set the tone for every client or employee who sat opposite her.

Shana made herself sit rather than pace and appear anxious when Julia arrived, but her foot bounced and her stomach continued to churn.

"Hello, Shana," Julia said from the doorway. "How are you?"

Hopeful. Scared. Excited. "I'm good, thanks. And curious."

Julia smiled. "Are you ready for your interview?"

"Yes." Shana stood. "Is there anything else you can tell me?"

"I prefer to let the client do the talking."

They left her office and headed to the consultation room two doors down, which held a conference table with chairs on either side. Shana had never been interviewed in that room before, had always been sent to the office or home of the client. It rattled her a little. Plus, the client came from Chance City....

Hope scattered as a man stood—a tall, lean, muscular, *familiar* man with laser-blue eyes and medium brown hair. Landon Kincaid. Shana had known him for about a year, disliked him for about that long, too—ever since he'd tried to steal her sister away last year from the man she'd always been meant for. He didn't seem to like her much, either.

"Hello, Shana," he said, not offering his hand to shake.

"Kincaid."

"I'll leave you two to talk," Julia said, shutting the door behind her.

Shana stared at the closed door for a few moments, gathering her thoughts, tamping down her disappointment. Would she ever learn not to hope? "We don't have to go through with the interview," she said as she turned to face him.

"Why not?"

"Well, now that you've seen it's me Julia lined up..." She shrugged.

"I asked specifically for you," Kincaid said, gesturing her to a chair.

She frowned. "Why?"

"You have all the skills I require."

Her head started to pound with confusion. She rubbed her temples and sat across from him. "Why didn't you just ask me directly? I saw you four days ago at Aggie's Thanksgiving dinner."

"I knew you'd say no." He sat. "This way you know it's strictly business."

"Why would I say no to a decent job offer? You know my situation. To have the opportunity to work in town is a dream come true. You could've skipped the agency fees and paid me the whole amount. I'd be better off for it."

"You would've said no," he repeated, smiling slightly, knowingly.

"Just because we don't like each other very much doesn't mean I wouldn't want the job."

He leaned back, studying her. "I take it Julia didn't fill you in on all the details."

She frowned. "She told me it was in Chance City and long-term."

"She didn't tell you it's a live-in position?"

Shock stabbed her, almost paralyzing her. "She did not. And I have a place to live, thank you very much." He knew that, of course, since he owned the building and, therefore, her apartment on the second floor.

"Actually, you don't. Or won't. I need a place for Dylan to live. He could afford the apartment you're in."

Shana stood so fast her world tilted. "*You're evicting me?* I have a seventeen-month-old daughter. Where are Emma and I supposed to live?"

"With me."

She couldn't believe this was happening. Just when her life had settled down. She had a routine. She'd earned people's trust again. Yes, she'd had to accept some help along the way, but as little as possible, and only for her daughter's sake.

Shana had caused enough controversy by running away years ago. She'd atoned. Now she wanted to be accepted and respected. Moving in with Kincaid, no matter how innocently, wasn't the way to accomplish that.

She headed to the door. "You wasted your time. And mine."

He beat her there, putting a hand on it to stop her.

Her heart pounded as his chest grazed her shoulder. She was hurt, angry and…something else she didn't want to identify. "Don't be childish, Kincaid."

"I'm asking you to hear me out."

Shana fought tears—of frustration, of exasperation, of despair. She couldn't seem weak in front of him.

"Please, Shana."

"Fine," she muttered after a minute. "But only because of Julia. I don't want to tell her I refused the job without having listened to what it actually is."

Kincaid stepped away, giving her space, keeping an eye on her in case she made a run for it, after all. He watched her raise her chin and return to the chair, where she plunked herself, crossed her arms and gave him a steady, cool, green-eyed stare. That expression wasn't unusual for her, but the way she'd tamed her long blond hair into a tidy ponytail was. She looked more professional than he'd ever seen her, especially wearing a skirt and jacket, and even high heels. He'd rarely seen her not wearing boots, jeans and a T-shirt that skimmed her slender frame.

He would've pulled up a chair next to her, but figured she wanted the distance of the table between them.

"Here's what I need," he said. "My businesses are booming. I don't have time for the personal attention I used to be able to give my clients."

"I thought that was why you hired Dylan."

"I hired Dylan because he needed a place in the world, but he's an eighteen-year-old apprentice. I spend a lot of time teaching and mentoring him. Eventually that's going to pay off. He's learning construction and contracting from the bottom up, but he's got a long way to go—years. In the meantime, details are not getting handled. That's where you come in."

"What details?"

"Sarah McCoy left for college in September. She'd been my housekeeper for two years—personally and professionally. I haven't found anyone reliable to replace her."

"I can handle that without moving in, Kincaid."

He could tell by the way her body moved that she was bouncing her foot under the table, her habit when she was annoyed. "I don't have time to take care of myself, either. I'm eating out all the time. The house gets cluttered. I don't like clutter. Laundry piles up."

"Those are basic household chores," she said. "It's not enough to keep me busy all day—and evening.

One day a week, maybe. If this is some kind of charity you're offering me—"

"I need help," he said, interrupting her before she launched into a speech about how she didn't need anyone's help, when, in fact, she did. He'd learned it from a reliable source, her sister, Dixie, who happened to be a good friend of his. It didn't matter that Dixie was on the other side of the world honeymooning and working. She'd gotten a call from Aggie McCoy after Thanksgiving telling Dixie how stressed-out Shana was, how even counting every penny still left her in the hole every month and how she'd fallen into Aggie's comforting arms and cried.

Dixie, in turn, had called him, asking if he could help Shana in some way. She would never take money from him, but could he give her work to do?

"Busywork?" Kincaid had asked Dixie.

"It can't seem like it. And if you even hint that you're doing this out of charity, she'll be out of there in a flash, and we just got her home, you know? She could run like a rabbit to who knows where, just like before. Plus there's the baby to think of. You'd have to handle it carefully. And you have to swear you'll never let her know I asked you for help."

"Here's the deal, Shana," he said now, looking at her cool expression. "Renovation is my primary work, but I also own thirty-two properties in the area. Not just in Chance City, but in surrounding communities. Tenants come and go, so places need cleaning and repairs have to be coordinated. I also need office help, especially with spreadsheets for expenses and taxes. I've got a box with a year's worth of receipts that need to be entered. Is that something you can do?"

"I'm good at math."

Which didn't really answer his question. "Your salary for the work you do for my business will feed through the agency. Beyond that, I'll give you room, board and a stipend for maintaining my home and, consequently, my life." He closed his hands into fists, fighting frustration. Dixie had warned him she would balk. "Frankly, I never wanted to be this busy. I've turned down more work than I've accepted through the years. But with Dylan involved now, it's different."

"How?"

"He needs the experience, the variety of work, so that he'll learn enough to be valuable, and eventually independent. I don't have the time to spend on frivolous things like cooking and cleaning." He met her gaze, noted how closed she still looked. "But I haven't told you the best part—at least for you, I think. I know you want to make a name for yourself in interior design. You'd be part of the package I offer to clients—design help. Not just for the remodeling itself, but for suggestions on how to decorate. You'd be the idea person, and I'd put your ideas into action. We'd make a strong team."

She finally looked interested. The deep furrow between her eyebrows smoothed out, at least.

"Design work for homes *and* businesses?" she asked.

He nodded, then he hoped to seal the deal when he said, "That part of the business is strictly yours. You keep what you earn." As the saying went, it was an offer she couldn't refuse, and he knew it. "You could probably accrue enough money in a year or two to afford a place of your own, not to mention gathering a client list, something you don't have yet since you're new to the design trade."

"Why are you doing this?"

A big reason why he'd agreed to Dixie's plea was because of his own past. He rarely thought about it anymore, and gave her only the barest details now. "When I was sixteen, I had to emancipate myself so that I could get away from a very bad situation. I didn't have a child to provide for like you do, but it was a long, hard road to success regardless. I mostly did it myself, but a few individuals helped me stay afloat, maybe even alive, those first years. I'm paying it back through Dylan, and now you, I hope." He leaned toward her. "You have pride. I get that, Shana. But don't let it stand in the way of the opportunity."

Pride had driven him for a long time, too.

"Emma's seventeen months old," she said hesitantly. "It's a busy, noisy age. Children create clutter."

Frankly, he hadn't given that aspect of the deal a lot of thought. He'd wanted to help Shana, and therefore Emma, but the day-to-day sharing of space with a toddler hadn't been part of his thinking. "I'm sure it'll be fine," he said. "My house is large, as you know."

"Actually, I don't know. I've never been there. I've never heard anyone talk about being invited there."

"I want that to change." The hermit life had suited him for years, but lately he'd been thinking it was time to embrace his town and its people, not one-on-one as he had for the nineteen years since he'd moved there, but within the entire community. It would help Dylan, too.

"If you're there to help," he said, "it *will* change. I've never even decorated for Christmas. Maybe that could be your first job. Emma would like that, wouldn't she?"

He hadn't intended to reel her in with a tug on her emotions, but apparently he had. He saw her expression change, softening even more. She wasn't the same angry, prideful woman as she was when she'd first come into the room. Her daughter would have a Christmas tree. Some things were worth swallowing your pride for.

"Yes," Shana said softly. "She would like that."

"She'd have her own bedroom, too. I figure you've been sharing with her. So, what do you say?"

A long pause ensued, then she said, "I need to think about it."

She'd totally caught him off guard. He'd been so sure…

"How much time do you need?" he asked. Really, what choice did she have? Finding affordable housing would be nearly impossible. Why was she stalling?

She stood. "I'll stop by your house tonight, if you're going to be home."

"Anytime after seven." He followed her to the door, opening it for her.

She didn't say goodbye but walked straight out of the office, not even stopping to talk to Julia. Bemused, he went to Julia's office.

"All settled?" she asked, welcoming him in with a gesture.

"She's thinking it over."

Julia's brows raised, then she smiled. "I've always admired her spirit."

"What you call spirit, I call stubbornness."

"I'm guessing you two tend to clash."

"We always have. I don't know why, but she took an immediate dislike to me." Because of that he hadn't warmed to her, either. Plus, she was just prickly.

"So, why hire her, especially to live in your house?"

Why, indeed? There was the favor to Dixie, which had also coincided with the fact that Dylan needed to be on his own. And he had some sympathy for Shana's situation, as well.

"I expect the time will come when she can manage fine on her own, Julia, but for now, she needs someone, and I have the means to help." He went to shake her hand. "I'll give you a call when I have her answer."

"Sounds good."

He took the stairs to the ground floor and walked to the parking garage. It had started raining since he'd arrived, which meant Shana would be making the hour drive up to their foothill community on wet roads. Her car was held together with baling wire and hope. He didn't like the idea of her—

He stopped the thought. He'd be a few minutes behind her and would see if she'd had to pull over.

As it turned out, he came up behind her before he'd driven fifteen minutes. He stayed there, going the damn speed limit, annoyed at her for it. Which was entirely unreasonable, he knew, but she generally annoyed him without making much effort to do so.

She also stirred him up, had since day one, but the only thing they seemed to have in common was that they both worked hard. His efforts had paid off. Eventually hers would, too. He admired her for trying to make it on her own, but if she hadn't had Emma, he never would have made Shana the job offer, Dixie's friendship or not. Emma would be their buffer. How much could anyone argue in front of a child? He knew firsthand the result of that. It did no one any good.

It was a lot to ask of one so young—being the reason to keep peace between two adults who didn't like each other much.

But it was the only way he could see this situation working out.

Shana drove home at exactly the speed limit. Every few seconds she looked at her rearview mirror, hoping Kincaid would pull around her and leave her in peace. She needed to think. His being on her tail interfered with that.

If this was the kind of employer he would be, she'd have to say no. She didn't need supervision or pressure in order to do a job well.

By the time she reached her exit to Chance City, she was beyond irritated, so when he exited right behind her, she pulled over. So did he.

"Are you having car trouble?" he asked, coming up to her as she got out of her car.

She plunked her fists on her hips. "Why are you following me?"

He looked surprised. "Following you? I was driving to the same place, and I figured it was rude to pass you."

She didn't know if he was telling her the truth or pacifying her.

"Are you mad at me, Shana?"

The way he angled toward her, almost intimately, lowering his voice a bit, threw her off, but she stood her ground.

"I can't believe you're kicking me out of my apartment."

"Technically, it's your sister's apartment."

She frowned. "I clean her spa business downstairs in trade for the rent."

"But who writes the rent check?"

"Dixie does, because her name is on the lease."

"She doesn't have a lease on the apartment, only on the spa." He gave her a sympathetic look. "Do you think the number of hours you work covers what she pays me in rent?"

"That's what she told me." She looked away, tallying up the numbers. "Probably not," she said finally, quietly. More charity to pay back…someday.

He didn't say anything.

"Would you really evict me?" she asked.

He seemed to dig deep for patience. "Shana, I'm offering you a chance to do the work you've been wanting to do. I'm offering you a home with a yard for your daughter to play in, and the opportunity to make enough money that you could save for a down payment on a house of your own in time. No," he said as she started to speak. "No, I wouldn't evict you. Dixie would never speak to me again. But why would you let this chance pass you by?"

There it was at last—the truth. "So you're doing this because of Dixie?"

He shoved his hands through his hair, fully regretting his decision now. "I'm doing this because I need help, and you fit the bill."

"What will people think, me living with you?"

"Do you really care?"

"Yes. And you should, too."

"I give up," he said, walking—stalking—away. "Forget the whole thing."

Shana saw her future flash before her eyes. "No, wait!" She rushed after him. "I'll take the job, on one condition."

"This should be good."

She almost laughed at his sarcasm. "You have to start dating."

He stared at her, as if shocked. "How do you know I'm not?"

Good point, especially since he'd said it so fast. "You have to start *visibly* dating. Or, at least bring your girlfriend to the Stompin' Grounds on Saturday night or something. No one has ever seen you date."

"Because I keep my private life private."

She crossed her arms. "Take it or leave it. I don't want people to think we're living together for any reason other than business ones."

"So, I should lead some woman on instead? Make her think I'm dating her because I'm interested, even if I'm not?"

She despised his logic, especially when she was too emotional to counter it, so she just looked him in the eye and waited. She needed a guarantee from him, although she wasn't sure whether she could trust it. He hadn't hesitated to go after her sister, after all.

"All right, Shana," he said at last. "I'll date. In public."

"The first Saturday night after I move in."

"Okay."

He said it too easily, as if he was already dating someone. "And you have to look cozy."

He laughed finally. "What I do on a date isn't yours to command. I'll show up with a woman at the Stompin' Grounds on Saturday night. That's all I'll promise."

She decided not to press. He'd already conceded more than she expected, so she stuck her hand out. "Deal."

His large, callous, warm hand engulfed hers. They'd never touched before. Bolts of lightning zapped her. He was a strong man. It would be easy to lean on him.

But she wouldn't. Not now. Not ever. She would just do her job and be grateful. Thanks to Kincaid, she wouldn't be anyone's charity case anymore.

Chapter Two

Shana pulled up in front of Aggie McCoy's house, turned off her engine and just sat, letting her nerves settle. Aggie had become Shana's rock in the year since she'd returned to town. Aggie was also Shana's key to success. If she could convince Aggie this was strictly a business deal, word would spread through town and no one would start speculating—or placing bets, a common occurrence.

Shana released her death grip on the steering wheel and headed toward the house and the woman who'd become her refuge. Sixty-nine years old and widowed for over twelve years, Aggie defined the title "Mother," having raised eight children, who'd given her a whole lot of grandchildren to love. She tended to mother just about everyone who crossed her path, related or not.

Plus she gave great big, cushy hugs that Shana's mother never seemed able to do.

That wasn't important now, she reminded herself. She had Emma, the only thing that mattered.

Shana knocked twice then opened Aggie's door. The scent of apples and cinnamon greeted her. Had she made pie or strudel? "Anybody home?" she called out.

"Mama! Mama!" Emma came running out of the kitchen and straight to Shana, who scooped her up and swung her around, her fine blond curls flying behind her, her Callahan green eyes a perfect match for her frilly T-shirt.

"Here's my baby girl. Something smells good."

"Apple. Mmm."

"You're early," Aggie said, coming into the room, wiping her hands on her apron. "How'd it go?"

Shana cuddled Emma, who toyed with her pendant. "I got the job. Full-time, right here in town."

"So, who's the boss?"

"Kincaid."

Aggie's black-penciled brows shot up. "Doing what?"

"Jill-of-all-trades. Housekeeper, property cleaner, office help, designer."

"Sounds like more than forty hours a week." Aggie headed toward the kitchen. "I need to take my pie out. Come on back."

"I'm not sure about the total hours, but it's a mixed bag of work. And it's live-in."

Aggie spun around but, uncharacteristically, said nothing.

"It's all on the up-and-up, Aggie. He needs my apartment for Dylan, and he needs a housekeeper, so Emma and I are moving in with him. This little peapod will have her own room for the first time, and a yard to play in." She rubbed noses with Emma, who flattened her hands on Shana's cheeks and gave her a big, wet kiss. "He's also dating someone."

"Is he, now?" Aggie pulled the apple pie out of the oven and set it on a metal trivet.

Shana inched closer. "I want people to know this is all business. Can you make sure that happens?"

"Are you accusing me of spreading rumors?"

"I'm thinking this is more like damage control. I've worked hard to get this town to accept me again. And there are never any rumors about Kincaid. This is a great opportunity for me. I can even afford to pay you and all the other babysitter volunteers for watching Emma."

"We'll talk about that some other time. I'm happy for you, honey. It sounds like a real good solution to all your problems. That Kincaid. He must have a crystal ball, hmm? He sure came up with a solution just when you needed it the most."

She gave Shana an odd look, as if she knew something Shana didn't know. "Things happen when they're supposed to. Isn't that what you always say?"

"That, and timing is everything."

There was a twinkle in her eye that made Shana wonder if she'd known what Kincaid was going to offer. "Will you try to squelch any rumors that pop up, Aggie? Please?"

"I'll try, honey, but you know the town has a life-blood of its own when it comes to other people's business. Somebody's bound to start a pool or two."

Shana had known that, of course. She'd just hoped otherwise. "Well, maybe when they see Kincaid's girl-friend, they'll change their minds."

"I find it interesting that he's never showed up with a girlfriend before but you think he will now."

"Me down," Emma said.

Shana took advantage of the moment to formulate an answer. "I do, too, but he told me he would be taking her to the Stompin' Grounds on Saturday night."

"Really?" Aggie chuckled. "I haven't been there in years. But why would he ask you to be his live-in housekeeper if he's finally serious enough about a girl to bring her to the town's hot spot and show her off? Wouldn't having you and Emma around cramp his style with a girlfriend?"

"Who knows how Kincaid's mind works." Shana crouched next to Emma as she pulled plastic containers out of a cabinet.

"When are you moving in?"

"By the weekend, I think. The apartment furniture belongs to Dixie, so I'm going to leave it for Dylan, although I may edit a little to make it more suitable for an eighteen-year-old guy. It's pretty feminine now. I really only have clothes and Emma's things. A few box loads, probably."

"Kincaid's got that big ol' pickup, so I figure you don't need me to help."

"No, but thank you. Here, Emma, stack these up and put them away. We need to get going." Shana stood. She touched Aggie's shoulder. "I was so embarrassed for crying all over you at Thanksgiving, but maybe finally saying it out loud, putting it out there into the universe, is what made Kincaid's offer happen."

Aggie nodded seriously. "I'm thinking you're right about that."

"Because *you* didn't tell him, right?"

She held up a hand. "I swear I didn't say a word to Kincaid." She swept Shana into her arms. "This'll be good for you and the little one."

Shana relaxed into her, eyes stinging. "I just want people to forget who I was before. I've grown up a lot since I left home, but especially this last couple of years."

"Honey, if rumors or betting pools get started, it would be because they like you. If they didn't, you wouldn't be worth their time."

Shana straightened. "I hadn't thought about it like that."

Aggie patted Shana's cheek. "There you go. If you've got time, you could stay for lunch. The pie will be cooled enough to eat after that. And maybe Emma could take her nap here, and you could get started packing."

Everything was happening so fast, Shana almost couldn't take it all in. But Aggie had allayed some of her fears, and there was the excitement of the work ahead of her.

Maybe she was a late bloomer, but blooming she was—finally—and she owed it all to Landon Kincaid, a man who'd always seemed to just tolerate her. Opportunity really could come from the strangest places—or people.

Hours later, Kincaid had just pulled up in front of the Take a Lode Off Diner to meet Dylan for dinner when his cell phone rang. He glanced at the screen first, let it ring once more then answered. "I've been expecting your call, Aggie."

"Oh, have you now? Why would that be?"

"I figure Shana already told you about my job offer."

"She did. Dixie must've called you because I told her I was worried about Shana."

"I promised Dixie I wouldn't tell Shana how I learned about her situation. You're the only other person who knows, who might guess at my motives."

"I'll take it to the grave, Kincaid."

He relaxed. "Thank you. She's proud."

"That she is."

"And she can get plenty angry," he added.

Aggie laughed. "Yes, but she's also worried about her reputation, too."

"I'm aware of that."

She didn't answer immediately. "If I were you, I'd let it be known right away what's going on. If you try to hide it at all, it's only going to work against you in the long run."

"Who should do the telling?"

"You, I think. You might start with Honey. Word'll spread from there, but it won't be malicious."

Honey owned the diner he was about to enter. That was easy enough. "Thanks, Aggie. For everything."

"You're welcome." Before she hung up, she said, "You know there's something between the two of you, Kincaid."

"Yeah. Animosity."

Aggie laughed a little. "There's that, of course, but for all that she seems like one tough cookie, she really has a tender soul. Been hurt a lot. Worked hard to recover. Independent as they come. Got it?"

"Don't mess with her," he said. "Yes, I got it."

"Okay, then."

He ended the call then put one through to Shana. "Aggie advises us to be up front about everything," he said when she answered. "She says we should start at the Lode, with Honey. Now, I can do it myself, or you could join me and Dylan for dinner and we could sort of announce it together."

"I'm fine with you taking on that task. If I'm there, we'll seem like a couple."

"Okay." He was both relieved and apprehensive. He just wanted to get it over with. The diner was a microcosm of the town. The initial reaction would represent how everyone felt. "When will you be ready to move?"

"Friday."

Four days from now. He wondered why she was stalling. She'd already told him she didn't have much to pack. "How about Saturday, instead? I book as few jobs as possible on weekends."

"Works for me. Have you lined up a date for Saturday night?"

"I'm thumbing through my black book as we speak." She laughed.

"Do you need boxes?" he asked.

"I'm good, thanks. I called Dixie to fill her in, but I had to leave a message and she hasn't called back. Have you talked to her?"

"We email about the house now and then." Not only were he and Dixie connected through business, he'd been remodeling and expanding Dixie and Joe's house for months while they were honeymooning and working overseas.

"I'll try her again later. Um, would you ask Dylan to call me, please?" she asked. "We can set up a time for him to stop by the apartment and see what he'd like changed to suit him."

"Sure." He saw Dylan pull up in his Kincaid Construction truck. "I'll stay in touch during the week, Shana. Let me know if you need anything."

"I'd like to see your house before I move in. Figure out what I need to buy for our bedrooms."

"How does tomorrow evening suit you?" They finalized their plans, then he ended the call and walked to where Dylan was parking.

"Hey, boss!" Dylan called out as he hopped down from the pickup.

"How'd the bathroom demo go?"

"All done."

They went through the diner door. "Even the tub?" Kincaid asked.

"Room's down to the studs. Found a few spots of dry rot."

"How'd you get the tub out on your own? The thing weighed a ton."

Dylan grinned. "Guess I'm stronger than you." He jabbed Kincaid in the arm and danced around as if boxing.

It was hard to believe that until two months ago the kid had been homeless. He'd already packed about fifteen pounds onto his six-foot frame, but still didn't weigh over one-fifty. He kept his hair a little long, and girls had started giving him the eye.

Kincaid waved at Honey, then they grabbed seats in the only open booth.

"Be right there, boys!" she called out, a plate in each hand, her long salt-and-pepper braid swinging side to side behind her.

"Eric called today," Dylan said. "He and Marcy are coming up to see Gavin and Becca on Saturday. They invited me for lunch." He looked away, his attention caught by four girls at a far booth who were sneaking glances at him and giggling.

Eric and Marcy Sheridan had rescued Dylan from the streets a couple months back. Eric's sister, Becca, had recently married Shana's brother, Gavin. Almost everyone in Chance City seemed to have a family connection to someone else.

Dylan dragged his gaze back to Kincaid. "Anyway,

do you have something lined up for me on Saturday or is it okay if I have lunch with them?"

"You're going to be a little busy on Saturday."

Disappointment dulled his eyes, but Kincaid knew he wouldn't argue about it. Dylan was grateful for the job, and more responsible than most eighteen-year-olds.

"You're going to be moving," Kincaid said, timing his words to coincide with Honey coming up to get their orders.

"Moving? Where? Why?" Dylan asked.

"Into the apartment above Respite."

Dylan frowned. "That beauty shop place downtown?"

"It's a salon, yes, but also a day spa. There's a nice one-bedroom above it."

"Where's Shana going?" Honey asked.

"I hired her through At Your Service to work for me. I need a housekeeper, for one thing, but more than that, Shana is perfect for the job."

Honey's brows rose. "Isn't that interesting."

"It's not personal, Honey. It's strictly business."

"I get an apartment all to myself?" Dylan asked, his eyes wide.

"Yes. It's a building I own, so you'll be paying me rent. I figure you've been freeloading off me for long enough."

Dylan's grin lit up the space.

"So…Emma, too, I suppose," Honey said.

"Of course."

"I've never seen you interact with a little one before."

Probably because he hadn't. He didn't have an opinion on children one way or the other, but he also wasn't going to be taking care of her. "I think she'll enjoy having a yard to play in," he said to Honey. "And I know Shana's happy not to be commuting to Sacramento. It's a good fit for everyone."

Kincaid's nerves settled some. Honey had reacted to the news, but she didn't turn around and announce it to the crowd to egg on some bigger reaction. She would spread the word without fanfare, he figured.

Kincaid and Dylan ordered their dinners and talked about what it would mean for Dylan to have his own place, and all the responsibilities it entailed. Kincaid wasn't sure Dylan was completely ready for the move, but it was the only way Kincaid could help Shana—at least, that she would accept. He'd keep a close eye on Dylan, make sure he didn't flounder in his independence. Being homeless and forced to fend for himself was different from living in an apartment alone, where there were more temptations, not just a need to survive.

"Can we go see the place?" Dylan asked as Kincaid was paying the bill a while later.

"Not tonight. She said you should call her, though, and come over so she can help you redecorate a little. It's kinda girly right now, I guess."

The four teenage girls walked past them, each one smiling at Dylan. Kincaid had lived on his own at sixteen. He knew the potential hazards of it, especially when it came to the opposite sex. "We'll need to have a birds-and-bees talk," he said.

Dylan rolled his eyes.

"If you're as smart as I think you are, you'll pay attention to what I have to say," Kincaid said.

"Yes, *sir.*"

Kincaid laughed at the military tone of voice.

They headed toward the diner door. "So, Shana's moving in, huh?" one customer asked.

"To work for me," Kincaid said, not stopping to engage in conversation. Fortunately, he'd never given the town reason to gossip about him through the years. He'd dated women outside of town, asked a fair price for the work he did and completed jobs on time. Still, even after nineteen years as a member of the community, he wasn't well-known enough to be kidded much.

Which might change now that he'd shaken up his predictable world.

"What's the big deal about Shana moving in as your housekeeper?" Dylan asked after they'd left the diner. "Lots of people have live-in help."

"She's a young, attractive, single woman, and this town loves its gossip." Kincaid pulled out his keys and toyed with them. "Remember that. And its citizens have long memories, too. It's like one big family, with its rivalries and devotion."

"Thanks. I'll remember." Dylan looked around. "You know, when you first offered me the chance to come up here and work, I really wanted the job but I wasn't sure about being so far from city life. But now I like it. It's old, you know? I love knowing that gold miners settled the town all those years ago, and that the downtown is just a couple of blocks long and has wooden sidewalks that make noise when you walk on them, and people say hello all the time."

"Even if everyone knows your business?" Kincaid asked.

"People knew who I was right away. That was cool. Plus, I like all the trees and hills and the great view of the Sierras. I can see myself staying here forever."

Chance City did get into one's blood, Kincaid thought. He'd felt the same affinity for it when he'd landed here. "You're right. It's a good town. See you at home."

Home. Kincaid's quiet home had been disrupted by having Dylan live with him, and it was about to be disrupted more. Much more. On the other hand, it should be more organized, too, having Shana around to take over some of his responsibilities. That much was the truth.

He just had to make sure she never found out why he'd offered her the job. He couldn't be responsible for her running away again.

For someone who'd built his reputation on being a man of his word, that would be a death knell to him.

Chapter Three

Kincaid's house was set back from the street by at least a hundred feet. Shana maneuvered her car down the long, curving driveway surrounded by pine and oak trees of varying heights and density, which mostly blocked the house from view, at least low to the ground.

"Sure is dark," she said, then made the final turn and stopped in front of a large lodgelike structure, with a well-lit front porch.

"Dark," Emma said from her car seat.

"I'll bet it's pretty during the day, though. What do you think, peapod? Look at all those windows. The view must be spectacular."

Emma babbled her response, although "pretty"—her newest word in her rapidly expanding vocabulary—

came through loud and clear mid-paragraph, even if it did sound more like "pity."

Shana got Emma from the backseat and headed up the stairs of the impressive structure, so suited to its environment. According to Aggie, he'd built the house himself about four years ago. Apparently everyone had talked about it, because his original goal had been to sell it, then he hadn't, surprising them all. They'd wondered why one man would need a house with five bedrooms. There'd even been a pool going for a while about when he would get married, but it never happened, and the gossip eventually died off, although everyone had wondered if he'd had his heart broken by a rejection.

Kincaid opened the front door and said hello before she could knock. He wore jeans, a plaid flannel shirt and thick socks. His shirtsleeves were rolled up a few turns, revealing muscular forearms. *Strong.* She associated the word with him more than any other.

"Cat got your tongue?" he asked, cocking his head.

"Kitty?" Emma asked, looking around. "Me down," she said, wriggling. "Kitty." Her tone was the same insistent one she used to say "cookie."

"There's no kitty, peapod," Shana said. "Or is there?"

"No pets at all," Kincaid said. "Come in out of the cold. I built a fire. Don't worry. It's got a large, sturdy screen. I made adjustments to it today to affix it to the stone. There's no danger to Emma."

His consideration caught her off guard. "That's very thoughtful of you."

"Well, selfish, too," he said. "I like my fires in winter

and didn't want to give them up." He turned to Emma. "How are you, Miss Emma?"

"Do you remember Kincaid, Emma?" Shana asked. "Can you say Kincaid?"

Emma shook her head, her thumb stuck firmly in her mouth.

"It's a new word, isn't it? Please try, Emma. Say Kincaid."

She gave Kincaid a long look, then said, "Kinky."

Shana slapped a hand over her mouth, stifling a laugh. "Almost, baby. Try again. Kin*caid*."

"Kin*ky*," Emma said, louder.

"Kinky it is," Kincaid said, not seeming bothered by it.

"If it's any consolation," Shana said, "she started calling Dylan 'Dilly.'"

"I'd rather be Kinky than Dilly."

"I'm sure." She smiled. "Where is he, anyway?"

"He drove to Sacramento to buy some posters, which apparently you suggested for his new place."

"I don't think he's a wildflower-print kind of guy, do you?"

Kincaid shook his head. He led them toward the fireplace, which took up a good portion of one wall and was bracketed by floor-to-ceiling windows, triple-paned, he said, for temperature control. The furnishings were perfect for the lodgelike environment, overscale and masculine, and yet not so masculine as to feel sterile.

"Me down," Emma said again. Shana set her on the

floor, and she toddled closer to the fireplace, coming to a stop several feet from it. "Pretty."

Shana joined her, taking off her tiny jacket, as well as her own. Kincaid took both and hung them on a rack by the front door.

"Your home is beautiful," she said.

"Thanks. Would you like to see the rest?"

"Yes. Come on, Emma."

Emma went ahead of them, so they followed her lead. She took them through the dining area on the opposite side of the living room, which also had a stunning view, then into the most perfect kitchen Shana had ever seen, with maple cabinets, stainless-steel appliances, green-and-gold granite countertops and more cabinet space than one man could ever possibly use, even if he were a professional chef. She'd had jobs as a short-order cook in small towns several times to earn her keep, but she didn't consider her skills more than basic. Could the right kitchen inspire her to become better at it?

They moved on to two downstairs bedrooms, then upstairs to see two more bedrooms, an office and the master suite, which was about the same size as the one-bedroom apartment she currently lived in. Every room was completely and beautifully furnished. She looked at it all with a designer's eye and didn't see a need to change anything, which was a little disappointing. She'd been hoping her talents would be put to use at his house.

"You and Emma are welcome to use the two bedrooms downstairs or upstairs."

"Thanks. I'll think it over." She thought it would be a good idea to keep her distance from him, keep Emma's noise to minimal disruption, and yet she liked the security of being on the same floor.

"I need you to decide soon. Dylan and I will have to move furniture out of the right bedroom to make room for Emma's things."

"Okay. Did you have a professional designer?"

"I designed the house, but I hired a decorator to help furnish it. If you'd lived in town then, I would've hired you."

Shana studied him for a few seconds, then watched Emma, who was standing at the foot of his bed as if plotting how to climb up on it. "This is weird," Shana said.

"What's weird?" He crouched to give Emma a boost, but she moved sideways, out of reach. He looked over his shoulder at Shana.

"Us. This. We're not arguing. We always argue."

"I wouldn't call it arguing. No one ever shouts. Mostly it's just insults. And you usually start it."

Shana's mouth dropped open. "*I* usually start it? *You* just started it." She rushed forward to stop Emma, who'd grabbed the deep green duvet and was trying to pull herself up.

"I won't let her fall," Kincaid said, as if offended. He reached for Emma.

"No," she said.

"Emma," Shana said, caution in her voice

"No Kinky." She took off running, another recently

mastered skill, giggling all the way. Shana was hot on her heels.

He found them in his office, Emma holding on to his desk and moving away from Shana, giggling at the game. Her hands hit the computer keyboard, waking up the monitor, the sudden light startling her.

"You can't touch the computer, Emma," Shana said, turning to look at Kincaid. "I'm so sorry."

He realized then what was on the screen. A spreadsheet of his annual expenses that he'd intended to transfer to a flash drive. She'd glanced at the screen. Would she notice? It had a big heading, in bold. If she read it, she'd know he'd already computerized the work he'd told her he wanted her to do.

Then she wouldn't believe anything else he said—

"Here's the box of receipts I told you about. I pretty much just toss them in here all year, then deal with them at the end."

"I can manage that. I'm kind of surprised you're that disorganized, Kincaid. You don't seem like you would be."

"We all have our flaws."

"Yes, we do. Let's go, peapod," she said.

Kincaid blew out a breath then trailed them more slowly, gauging their location by following the laughter. There hadn't been much laughter in this house. Not that it was a depressing place to be, not at all, but he'd been alone most of the time. Having Dylan around had been an adjustment, and there had been laughs between them, but nothing like he expected would become the norm with Shana and Emma around.

Kinky. He wondered what people would say once they heard Emma call him that in public, if she ever warmed up to him. The idea that she wouldn't take to him hadn't crossed his mind. Until now.

Except, she was Shana Callahan's daughter, after all. Maybe like mother, like daughter.

He went into the living room and stoked the fire, adding a log, then sat in his chair, leaving the sofa for them. They came running back into the room, Shana scooping her up and whirling her around. It was a homey moment, one played out in houses around the world all the time, but a first for him. They were a family unit, Shana and Emma. Shana would be there day in and day out, taking care of the house, helping with his business, in his line of sight a great deal of the time, and sleeping nearby.

A wife but without the conjugal benefits, he thought.

He'd sort of considered that before, but having her here finally brought it home, the enormity of what he'd offered her—she'd be an almost wife.

And what she considered a negative—their sparring—he enjoyed. A lot. She was usually direct, her honesty startling at times, but he wished he knew why she was edgy around him. He hadn't noticed her having the same reaction or behaving the same way with anyone else.

"Baby girl, you are wet. You need your diaper changed," Shana said.

"Diappy."

"Exactly." Shana looked at Kincaid. "We should probably go. I'll change her at home."

But you just got here. He was caught between relief and disappointment. "Okay."

They put their jackets on. He followed them out the door and down the steps, waiting as Emma was buckled into her car seat.

"Say bye-bye to Kincaid," Shana said to her, not shutting the door yet.

"Bye-bye." She waved. "Kinky! Bye-bye!"

Apparently, she warmed up at the thought of leaving. "Goodbye, Miss Emma. I'll see you soon."

Shana shut the door, got in the car and started the engine. She rolled down the window, then she stared out the windshield, as if working up the nerve to say something.

Kincaid crouched and waited.

"Thank you for the job. And I'll try not to argue with you," she added with a small smile. "Not sure I can follow through on that one."

"Baby steps, Shana. Just be honest. That's all I ask."

"You, too," she said.

He tapped the car with his open hand to end the conversation, then stood. He could be honest with her—to a point. They both had reputations to uphold, after all. He intended to do just that. "It's cold. You should get going."

"See you Saturday," she said with a wave, then she was gone.

He watched until her taillights were out of sight. He didn't think he'd ever forget the look on her face as she'd thanked him. It had humanized her for him in a way that he hadn't acknowledged about her before. He'd been told she was well liked by many other people, but at times it was as if she'd gone out of her way for him not to like her.

Until now.

He was glad he'd seen it for himself. He saw hope, even that they could become friends through all this.

Time would tell.

Shana carried Emma up the stairs from the salon to her apartment. How tiny the place seemed after seeing Kincaid's. A few minutes ago, she'd almost told him about her past, but had stopped herself in time and only thanked him. A lot of people knew she'd moved around a lot, but not many other details. She hadn't wanted rumors to spread, especially since she'd already come back to town as a single mother.

Only her immediate family knew the circumstances—and Aggie. For all that Aggie loved a good bit of gossip, she'd kept Shana's situation to herself, even quoting her hero, Henry Ford—"'Failure is simply the opportunity to begin again, this time more intelligently.'"

Shana hoped she could live up to Aggie's expectations, and wished her parents had been as generous. They'd been much slower to put the past behind.

Maybe she was being too hard on them. Her mother had come a long way in forgiving Shana for leaving and also accepting her back, but Shana sometimes wondered if it was more because of Emma, not her. Her father, always the strong, silent type, still rarely spoke to her. He'd mostly been the reason she'd run away—him and her own rebellious nature.

She wanted forgiveness from her father for that. Since he wasn't one to share his feelings, she doubted she would ever hear those words from him.

"I love you, peapod," Shana said to her daughter as she set her down to change her.

Emma hadn't learned to say I love you, yet. Shana was looking forward to it. She didn't have any memories of her parents saying those words.

"How about a bath?" Shana asked.

"Bath!"

That was an enthusiastic yes.

After Emma had a splashy swim and two books read, Shana tucked her into her crib, then she fixed a cup of tea and sat down for what felt like the first time all day. Filled boxes were stacked in one corner of the living room, waiting to be taken to Kincaid's.

She closed her eyes and leaned her head against the sofa, then the phone rang. Her sister.

"Hey, Dix! It's 6:00 a. m. where you are."

"How do you do that?" Dixie asked with a laugh. "I always have to look at the clock and count the time difference on my fingers."

"We all have our talents."

"I guess we do, math whiz. I got your message, but Joe and I were out of cell phone range. What's up?"

"I have…interesting news. I got a job. A full-time, permanent position, right here in Chance City."

"That's wonderful! What is it?"

"I'll be working for Kincaid." Shana waited for her

sister's reaction. Dixie knew how Shana felt about Kincaid.

"Really? Is he hiring a bodyguard, too?"

Shana laughed. She missed her sister so much. If only they could be sitting on the sofa together, talking about this situation over tea. "Very funny, Dix."

"Well, there is the whole I-can't-stand-Kincaid thing you've had going since the day you met him. You two are like oil and water sometimes."

"I know, but it's a chance to make a good life for Emma and me. I can't turn that down."

"You really have grown up."

"I hope so. And some of that credit belongs to you. I couldn't have made it without you, Dix, and that's no exaggeration. But as grateful as I am, I can't continue to clean the salon. I'm not going to have enough time."

"What all are you going to be doing?"

"Everything. Helping with his business, drumming up design work, taking care of his home."

"His home?"

"I'm moving in. Emma and I will be living there."

There was a long stretch of silence. "Live-in? Really, Shana, is that wise?"

"I don't know yet. I guess I'll find out. But Dix, it means I can save money. In time I can have the life I've wanted for Emma and me."

"But...living together, Shana?"

"He hired me through At Your Service. It's all on the up-and-up." She sounded defensive, even to herself. "Look, I know it seems odd, but I'm getting used to the idea. I think it'll work out fine."

"What will Mom and Dad say?"

Shana wished she could say she didn't care, but it wasn't true. "They'll probably be embarrassed or offended. I can't change that."

"Well, you're an adult. You get to make your own decisions. As for the job at the salon, Jade could use the money, I'm sure. She'll take it on, as well as her receptionist duties." Dixie yawned, then laughed. "Sorry. We've put in long hours this week."

"You were supposed to be home by now. Eight-thousand miles from here to Tumari is way too far."

"I know. Oh, I'm so homesick, Shana. I'm aiming for Christmas in Chance City. I won't care if I ever travel again in my entire life, although I wouldn't have passed up this opportunity for anything. And Joe's really shined, you know? But he misses everyone, too."

They chatted a little longer then said good-night. Shana picked up her tea again and sipped it, although it had cooled. She considered reheating it, but her thoughts wandered instead.

Dixie had been gone for over six months. Had Kincaid gotten over her during that time? Or would having her home stir up old feelings? She understood what he'd seen in Dixie. She was smart and confident and beautiful, not to mention all those curves that men appreciated, whereas Shana was just…ordinary, and too thin, lacking curves. At least that should help in keeping things professional between her and Kincaid. Without physical attraction, it wouldn't be complicated.

She needed this job, and their relationship, to stay

uncomplicated. For her sake, for Emma's sake, for her chance at a happy life.

Nothing mattered more than that.

Kincaid had just said good-night to Dylan, who'd gone off to bed. They'd stayed up later than usual, Dylan too excited about moving into his own place to settle down, so they'd watched a movie and half of another before he yawned and headed to his room.

Kincaid couldn't settle down, either. Seeing Shana in his house, in his personal space, had been disconcerting. He'd thought since Dylan had been living there for a couple of months, and Kincaid had gotten accustomed to having someone around, that it wouldn't be difficult to have Shana and Emma move in.

Wrong. He'd hadn't foreseen how much time he'd be spending alone with a woman he found attractive, if not exactly the kind of woman he usually went for, the fun-loving, easygoing women he tended to ask out.

And then there was Emma. Not just busy but rambunctious. Curious.

His phone rang. It was late, too late for a casual call. Then he saw the caller ID.

He leveled out his voice. "Hello, Dixie."

"You're moving her in with you?" she almost shouted.

He winced a little. "You wanted me to help her. I'm helping."

"I did not ask you to move her into your house, Kincaid. I asked you to give her a job."

"You asked, and I quote, 'Can you please help her in some way?'"

"As in *give her a job*."

"I did that. Several jobs, actually, because I can't give her enough work for one full-time job, so I needed to improvise. I decided I could use a housekeeper more than anything. She won't have to pay rent, and she'll have money left over at the end of the week. Now, what's your objection?"

"If she finds out I had anything to do with this—"

"I already promised you she wouldn't. What else?" Because he knew there was more. He was just waiting for her to say it.

"You can't sleep with her, Kincaid."

"For the sake of argument, why not?" Because the idea wasn't as impossible as he'd thought a couple of days ago.

"Because you're not the marrying kind, and she needs a marrying kind."

"I think that's up to her, don't you? Anyway, that's not on my agenda. I thought you'd be happy. She'll be in a safe place with plenty to do, and leisure time, as well. No more commuting to Sacramento. A backyard for Emma. I think I hit the ball out of the park for you."

"I'll be keeping close tabs. I'll call her a lot."

"I'm sure she'll like that." He found himself grinning. Dixie could be almost as stubborn as Shana.

"So, I should just say thank you?"

"That would be nice. I've disrupted my life a lot for you."

"Thank you."

He laughed. "That didn't sound too sincere."

"I'm awaiting the outcome. I do appreciate that you are doing something for her. I'm just worried about exactly what that is."

"You trust me, or you wouldn't have asked," he said, taking the stress level down a few notches. "I'll do right by your sister."

"Thank you," she said, a genuine tone in her voice this time.

"You're welcome. Feel free to call and check anytime."

"I will."

He laughed then they hung up. Having Dixie find out about the live-in situation had been his biggest hurdle, and he'd jumped it.

You can't sleep with her. It hadn't been on his mind for the past year, yet suddenly the idea of it was there, circling him, burning the image in his head.

He was counting on the fact she would be difficult to live with, which would keep his libido under control. That, and Emma, who would be around all the time, too.

He should be in for one helluva time.

Chapter Four

Respite, Dixie's day spa, was like most hair salons or barbershops in small-town America—a place where advice was sought and dispensed, problems debated and solved, and gossip spread, true or speculative. As Kincaid pulled into the parking lot behind the building, Dylan in his truck behind him, he anticipated a small, curious crowd inside. There was no outside access to the apartment, so Kincaid and Dylan had no choice but to enter the female-occupied space. Kincaid and a few other men in town got their hair cut at Respite, but he saw only women today.

"Ladies," he said. "I'd like you to meet Dylan Vargas. He's the new upstairs tenant. Be gentle with him, okay?"

"Aw, Kincaid, you're no fun," Aggie McCoy said,

looking like some kind of alien, with foil sticking out from her head and black dye at her roots. "Dylan, have you met my granddaughter, Posey?"

"No, ma'am, I haven't." Dylan nodded to the cute teenager seated in a chair next to her grandmother, having her hair cut and looking embarrassed about the new boy in town seeing her looking less than perfect. Her cheeks flushed pink.

And so it begins, Kincaid thought, stopping short of heaving a sigh. *And he'll have a place of his own. Great....*

They'd had the birds-and-bees talk last night. Kincaid had been direct and graphic with the boy, because apparently his father never had been. Dylan was startlingly naive. Kincaid hoped he'd cured him of that. Being armed with information was a whole lot better than ignorance or guesswork.

"Posey's seventeen," Kincaid said as he and Dylan climbed the stairs a minute later.

"Got it," Dylan said.

Kincaid glanced back down and saw all the women watching them. "I think we'd better design a plan to move your entrance to the outside so you don't have to interrupt the clients in their private domain."

"Fine by me," Dylan said, sounding relieved.

The upstairs door was open, so they climbed the child gate and went inside. "We're here," Kincaid called out.

Emma came running. Kincaid crouched down in time to catch her as she neared, but she came to a quick stop, keeping her distance.

"Good morning, Miss Emma."

"No Kinky!"

Dylan laughed. "Kinky? Seriously?"

"Dilly up!" Emma said, raising her arms.

"Dilly? Seriously?" Kincaid said, feeling rebuffed as Dylan lifted her into his arms, looking only slightly uncomfortable at the nickname.

"Dilly, Dilly," she said, patting his face.

"Where's Mommy?" Kincaid asked.

Emma pointed. Shana had come up behind him.

"Good morning," she said. "I'm packed and ready to go, except that I haven't taken the crib apart. But first, Aggie brought some homemade apple turnovers for all of us."

She headed to the kitchen, and Kincaid found himself staring at her rear. She was slender but with curves in all the right places. Not that he hadn't noticed before, but he was finding himself more aware of her than he had been before.

Which probably wasn't a good thing.

As they dug into the turnovers they talked about the day's plan of attack. Load her possessions into Kincaid's truck, unload Dylan's and haul them upstairs, although he had few possessions. Then they would all head to Kincaid's to unload Shana's things and set up the crib.

They traipsed through the salon back and forth, back and forth, until everything was loaded and unloaded. Aggie offered to keep Emma, but Shana thought she should be part of the move. By seeing her crib set up in her new bedroom, she would more readily accept that she would be sleeping there.

"Do you think that's all it will take?" Kincaid asked as Shana buckled Emma in her car seat to head to his house. "She'll see her crib and that's that?"

"I don't think the house change will be a problem. She's been babysat by a lot of different people and is used to that. I think the biggest adjustment may come from me not sleeping in the same room with her."

"She, uh, doesn't have temper tantrums, does she?" he asked, suddenly wondering what he'd agreed to take on.

"Occasionally." She shut the car door and faced him. "I know this is going to be a big change for you, too."

She looked nervous, and he realized he wasn't the only one worried that they were getting into something neither was ready for. "You already warned me that she's busy."

"And noisy. Speak now or forever hold your peace."

He considered that for a moment. "A deal's a deal."

"I'll try to keep her away from you as much as possible," she said tightly.

She started to climb into the car, but he stopped her by putting a hand on her arm. The electricity of that one touch made him break contact immediately, and confused him.

"I don't expect you to keep her locked in her room. Just because I'm paying you a salary doesn't mean you can't consider my house your home, Shana. I don't want you to feel like a visitor. I figure I'll get married someday and have children. Emma will be good experience for me."

He'd been trying to make her relax, but her expression indicated he hadn't succeeded. She frowned in that way she had, where her lips pinched together and her nose wrinkled. He fought the sudden urge to kiss that frown away.

"If you have plans to get married, why did you invite me to move in?" she asked sharply.

"It's not like I have someone lined up at the door. I'm just saying that I'll probably want a family at some point. Can we leave it at that?" The truth was that he'd rarely thought about it, *especially* about having children. It had always seemed like something for the future, if ever. Then the years just continued to pass.

"Did you get a date for tonight?" she asked, not seeming appeased by his answer.

"I said I would."

"Who?"

"You don't know her."

"What's her name?"

She sounded a little angry or annoyed or something, which he couldn't figure out, since she was the one who'd demanded he take a date to the Stompin' Grounds tonight.

"Hey, boss! I've got to get to Gavin and Becca's for lunch, remember?" Dylan shouted. He was waiting in his truck, his engine running, to follow them and help unpack.

"We'll meet you at the house," Kincaid called out to

Dylan, then to Shana he said, "We can finish this another time."

A few minutes later they all pulled up at the house. Because Emma was already overdue for her morning nap, Kincaid and Dylan put the crib together first. Kincaid was aware of Shana coming in and out of the room with boxes. Emma sometimes followed her to the gated landing and sometimes stayed in the room, "helping." A Jack and Jill bathroom connected the two upstairs bedrooms. With both bathroom doors open, she had free range of the rooms.

He'd been a little surprised Shana had taken the upstairs rooms, close to his. He'd fully expected her to stay downstairs. It'd seemed easier with Emma, not having to go up and down stairs as much.

As Shana unpacked, Kincaid was hit by the responsibility of making sure Emma didn't get into trouble. He'd never had to watch where he put his tools before, and suddenly the realization of what could happen had him sitting back on his haunches and worrying.

"And you thought bringing *me* into your house was going to be a challenge to your hermit life," Dylan said as he tightened the final screw on his side of the crib. His eyes were sparkling.

"Yeah. What was I thinking?" Kincaid tried to joke back.

"Are you sure you can handle it?"

"It?"

"Having Emma around. For that matter, having Shana here. It doesn't take a psychic to see you got it bad for her."

Shana was making her way to Emma's bedroom through the bathroom when she heard Dylan's words. She stopped cold. Got it bad for her? She waited for Kincaid's response.

"Knock it off," he said. "You don't know what you're talking about."

Was that true? Shana wondered. She didn't want that. She wanted to do her job, and that was all. She'd told him from the beginning that everything had to be strictly business between them. She needed to be her own person. If he felt—

"Sorry," Dylan muttered.

Shana backed out the bathroom then walked in again making enough noise to alert them.

"Mama!" Emma called, running to her. "Night night."

"I'll bet you're tired, peapod. Are you hungry? Do you want to eat before you go to bed?"

"No." She said it defiantly, the way she always said no, but she tucked her head against Shana's neck.

"Is the crib about ready?" she asked, not looking at either of the men, uncomfortable now after Dylan's statement.

"All done," Kincaid said.

She walked up to Dylan. "Would you hold her for a second while I put the bedding on?"

"I'm already late," he said hesitantly, looking at Kincaid.

"I'll take her. You go ahead. Tell everyone I said hello."

"Me, too, please," Shana said, then she passed Emma

to Kincaid. Emma eyed him steadily, warily, but was tired enough not to fight it, apparently, although she didn't snuggle against him. Shana made up the crib quickly, the ladybug and butterfly bedding a familiar sight for Emma to wake up to, even if the room wasn't.

Shana felt Kincaid's eyes following her every move, but never looked at him, still confused—and maybe something else—about his wanting her. When she was finished, she reached for her sleepy-eyed daughter.

Emma barely made a sound while she was tucked in, then Shana and Kincaid left the room, leaving the door ajar a little, the baby monitor turned on. When they got to the top of the stairs, he stopped her.

"About what Dylan said, Shana."

Her heart plunged into her stomach. "How did you—"

"I saw you reflected in the bathroom mirror. Look, Dylan's got it all wrong, okay? I don't want you to tiptoe around me or think you've made a mistake. He's eighteen. He thinks he knows everything."

Disappointment blanketed her, even though she knew she should be glad. "Okay. Thanks." She took the stairs with some speed, needing to break eye contact. "Are you hungry? Can I fix you—us—some lunch?"

"I called in a pizza order. Should be here any minute."

Thoughtfulness was a trait Shana appreciated. And kindness. So far, he'd shown both, as well as a patience she'd never seen in him before—at least not with her.

It made her want to scream. Even though he'd said he didn't want their relationship to change, she found herself behaving differently. Like an employee, she thought, not an acquaintance. It didn't matter what he said, she knew if she didn't do the job well, he'd let her go. He was paying her, after all, not taking care of her.

Shana sighed at her own hypocrisy. When it came down to it, she didn't know what she wanted. She'd been living day-to-day for so long, she didn't know how to look ahead.

She really needed to start seeing the big picture.

They sat at the kitchen counter to eat their pizza, the view out the window spectacular, which made up for the fact that neither of them seemed to have much to say. She focused on the yard. Most of the oaks had lost their leaves, but a lot of green remained in the form of pine and cedar trees, and some holly bushes. After a few minutes of silence, she picked up her second slice and wandered to the window, getting a closer look, then spotted a children's play structure off to one side. It held two swings, a slide and a climbing ladder.

"Think Emma will like it?" Kincaid asked, coming up beside her.

"Did you put that in for her?"

He shrugged. "Kids need a place to play."

It took a few seconds for his words to sink in. He'd gone way out of his way for her. For Emma.

"Thank you." It was all she could manage to say. He kept surprising her.

He leaned a shoulder against the wall, studying her. "I set up an account for you at Angel's Market. You'll also have a Kincaid Construction credit card for business-related expenses, including gas. Card hasn't arrived yet."

"Okay. What kind of food do you like?"

"I'm pretty easy. Basic stuff, you know, meat and potatoes. Bacon and eggs. Sandwiches."

"That's good, because I'm kind of basic when it comes to cooking. Do you like salad? And soup?"

"Yes to both. Eventually you'll be busy with other jobs, so I don't expect a big meal every night. If you would just keep the refrigerator stocked and the household running as smoothly as possible, that's enough for me."

"I haven't noticed any of the clutter you said you had." In fact, the house was spotless. Knowing the way he worked—how he cleaned up his work site every day—she wondered if his house had ever been cluttered.

"Oh, um, yeah. Dylan and I picked up. I figured you should start with a clean slate."

She didn't believe him, which made her start to doubt other things he'd said.

"I think the weirdest thing for me," he said, not seeming to notice her silence, "is having someone else do my laundry."

"Do you wear boxers or briefs?" she asked.

He gave her a long look before he answered. "Briefs."

"There. The worst of it is over." She took another big bite of pizza. "So, who *are* you taking to the Stompin' Grounds?" she asked, changing the subject entirely.

"Her name is Jessica."

Jessica. Shana hated her already. Shocked at her reaction, she walked away, intent on cleaning up the kitchen, keeping busy. "Have you dated her a lot?"

"I'm not done with that," Kincaid said, pointing to the pizza as she flipped the lid shut to put it in the refrigerator.

"Sorry." She shoved the box toward him, then grabbed a pen and paper to make a grocery list, keeping herself busy.

She assumed the big bite he took instead of answering her question was a stall tactic. "Have you?" she asked. "Dated her a lot?"

He shrugged, obviously uncomfortable.

"What's the etiquette going to be for us, Kincaid? What do I do when you bring a woman over for dinner or to spend the night?"

"We'll cross that bridge when we come to it. For now, that's not in my plans."

"What about if I want to have a male friend overnight?" *Like that was going to happen anytime soon.*

"Is that something you do often?" he asked.

"I just want to know the rules."

He wiped his mouth with his napkin then wadded it up and dropped it on top of his plate. "I don't like rules much. Let's not put up barricades before we need to."

"What's your gut reaction?" She was pushing him for answers she probably didn't want to hear, but she was confused by his behavior. All they'd ever done was bicker—and he wasn't bickering anymore. What did it mean?

"My gut reaction is to say you can't bring someone

home overnight." He smiled grimly. "Aren't you glad you asked?"

She crossed her arms. "Why would you say no?"

"I don't think you'd be setting a good example for Emma."

"Is that the only reason?" She really should shut up, she thought. Why was she forcing him?

He cocked his head. "What do you want me to say, Shana? That I would be jealous? Is that what you want?"

"No."

"Would you be jealous if I had a woman stay overnight?"

"Of course not."

"Then what's the problem?"

He'd moved close to her, was only inches away, looking into her eyes as if he could read all her secret desires. And desire him, she did, suddenly, intensely. She wanted to grab him by the shirt, pull him close and kiss the daylights out of him.

Instead she spun around and turned on the faucet full force. "I don't know. I apologize. Goading you is a habit."

"Well, break it. We need to get along."

"You told me to be honest."

"Honesty is one thing. Provoking an argument is another."

She nodded, feeling like an idiot. It was exactly what she'd been doing. *I'm scared,* she wanted to say. *I don't know what to do about you. You confuse me.* But that was too honest.

"I need to run a few errands," he said. "Here's your house key. I'll see you later."

She didn't tell him goodbye, couldn't say a word. They hadn't gotten off to a good start, but that was entirely her fault.

Shana heard the front door shut. She finished cleaning up the kitchen then went upstairs to check on Emma, who slept soundly, even when Shana brushed her hair from her face and ran her fingers down her soft cheeks. She'd probably sleep for another hour, which gave Shana time to unpack her own clothes and put out her few knickknacks.

She looked around her new bedroom. The furniture was maple and much finer than she was used to. With some different art on the walls, she could make it her own and feminize it some. She didn't want to do too much, since she wouldn't be there forever. She'd never put down roots for long. Why would this time be any different?

When she was done putting away her possessions, she went back downstairs to finish up the grocery list. After Emma woke up and was fed, they could go to the store. She would make Kincaid a chocolate cake as an apology—

No, she couldn't. He was going out tonight. Because she'd insisted.

Which meant she and Emma would be alone. As usual.

Wasn't it funny how circumstances could change, and still be the same?

Chapter Five

The Stompin' Grounds was an old-time bar and grill that had survived a couple generations of pool-playing, dance-loving, beer-drinking residents of Chance City. It was dark, even during the day, kind of run-down, offered great bar food, and music, of course—a jukebox most of the time and live music on Saturday nights.

Kincaid wasn't a regular. Although he'd spent his junior and senior years of high school in town and been friends with a lot of people from his graduating class, he didn't socialize much. It had taken him a long time to recover from his life prior to moving here, which was pretty much a living hell. He hadn't wanted to explain his past to anyone, so he hadn't gotten close.

That had changed through the years. People invited him to barbecues and holiday dinners. He had friends, just not intimate friends. He confided in no one, but he was respected because of the way he ran his businesses, honestly and competently.

Until recently it was all he'd wanted. Now he hungered for more. Intimacy, in particular. A friend he could really talk to. Oh, he could hang out with one of the McCoy or Falcon brothers—they were all friends on some level, but they had each other, a brother bond that he didn't have. Or family of any kind, actually.

In a parking lot filled with pickup trucks, Kincaid was waiting in his own for Jessica to arrive. She'd insisted on driving up from Sacramento rather than his picking her up, which made sense, but he was kind of a throwback when it came to things like that. The man was supposed to pick up the woman for a date.

Not that this was a date, exactly. She was helping him out, that was all, but it still felt wrong to have her drive up on her own.

He spotted her baby blue Mercedes pulling into the lot and got out to meet her. Her car might be out of place at the Stompin' Grounds, but she'd dressed perfectly in skin-tight blue jeans, boots and a pink western shirt. Her hair was dark, short and stylish, her eyes deep blue, and her body well toned. She was one of the most successful Realtors in northern California, and when he'd branched off from his contracting work into real estate, she'd mentored him. He owed her a lot, yet here she was, doing him a favor.

"Hello there, gorgeous," she said, giving him a hug.

"Hello, yourself, beautiful." They'd almost slept together once, a few years back. She'd just ended a long-term relationship and needed to know she was still attractive. He'd never regretted talking her out of it.

"So, I'm supposed to hang all over you, hmm?" she asked as they headed toward the building.

He smiled. "Not exactly. Just look interested."

"Are you going to lay hands on me?"

"I plan to dance with you."

She slipped her arm through his. "Dancing can be incredible foreplay, darlin'."

"So I've heard." He'd forgotten what she was like when she turned on the charm. He usually saw her in business mode.

"I don't suppose they serve veggie burgers in this joint," she said as they reached the door.

"Probably not. Their hamburgers are amazing, however."

"Guess you'll have to dance off the calories with me. I'm finding it a lot harder these days to keep my girlish figure."

"Fishing for compliments, Jess?" He didn't know how old she was. Maybe forty. "We both know you're going to turn a lot of heads tonight."

She grinned over her shoulder at him as they went inside. "Will you get jealous and fight over me?"

The sudden rush of noise prevented him from answering, but her words took him back to his earlier conversation with Shana about jealousy. No, he wouldn't be jealous of Jess turning heads or even of her dancing with someone else. He'd never fought over a woman before. He'd seen enough fighting when he was growing up and preferred to use his wits to get him out of tight situations. But when it came to Shana? He felt differently, and he didn't like that.

"Table or bar?" he shouted to Jessica.

"Bar." Her eyes gleamed, taking it all in. The band was setting up. For the moment, the jukebox was at full volume and the conversation elevated to compensate for the noise.

He already wanted to go home.

Except he didn't want to get home until Shana was in bed, didn't want to answer any questions she might ask. She'd sent him off with a tensely cheerful goodbye. Tomorrow morning would be soon enough to face her.

Creating the job for her was coming back to haunt him already. He couldn't come and go at his own house anymore without Shana knowing the details of his life.

He and Jess made their way to the bar, found two seats then ordered a couple of beers and a menu.

"Do you know people here?" she asked.

His gaze swept the room. "Quite a few, yes." He also noted a great deal of interest in him—and his date, he assumed. He'd expected talk. That was the point of this whole exercise, after all, to get people talking about him and the woman he was with, not about Shana moving in.

Tom, the bartender/owner, set their mugs in front of them. Kincaid lifted his then stopped before it reached his mouth as he saw who'd just arrived.

"This should be entertaining," he muttered.

"What?" Jess asked.

"See the older couple that just came in? That's Aggie

McCoy, one of the town's matriarchs. She's the one we'll have to put on a show for."

"Who's the attractive man with her?"

"Doc Saxon. He used to be the only doctor in the community, but he recently retired." In fact, Shana's brother, Gavin, had taken over his practice. Small town, Kincaid thought. Small world. He and Gavin had gone to high school together. "My guess is that Aggie found out I was bringing a date here tonight, so she made Doc come with her."

"I don't know. She's flirting. I think she likes him."

Kincaid studied the couple. Aggie's husband had died years ago. Doc Saxon had been a widower for a while. They seemed like polar opposites, but when did that stop people?

Aggie headed straight to where Kincaid sat. "Heard you were gonna be here," she said, then stuck her hand out to Jess. "Hi. I'm Aggie McCoy, and this is Jim Saxon."

"Jessica Donnell."

"I never realized you had a first name," Kincaid said to Aggie's date with a wink. "Do we call you Jim now instead of Doc?"

The lean, fit, seventy-four-year-old, with only slightly graying hair and kind eyes, smiled. "I'll answer to either. I hear Shana and Emma have moved in with you."

"Shana's working for me. Emma came as part of the package."

"I see. Well, we'll leave you to your evening. Come on, Aggie. Let's find a table."

Aggie wasn't done socializing. They greeted everyone in the room before finally sitting near the jukebox.

"They give me hope," Jess said as her hamburger was set in front of her.

"Who?" Kincaid reached for the ketchup.

"Aggie and her doctor. They're smitten. Isn't that nice at their age?"

Kincaid still didn't buy it. Doc and Aggie had known each other forever. Why would their relationship suddenly change?

"Oh, man!" Jess said after taking a bite of her burger. "This is really good."

"Maybe it's just been too long since you've eaten one."

"Who cares? This was worth the drive."

"And I wasn't?"

She laid a hand on his cheek, looking to all the world like a tender gesture. "Since you won't sleep with me, the answer is no."

He laughed. He was enjoying himself, being out, listening to music, having dinner with a comfortable companion. The band started to play just about the time Kincaid and Jess finished eating, and they made their way to the small dance floor. Although the music was fast, they might as well be slow dancing, the space was so crowded.

He noticed Jess eyeing the pool table. More specifically, eyeing Big Dave Gunderson, a lumberjack of a man who owned a successful towing business and cleaned up well after hours. He and Jess were about as opposite as Aggie and Doc, Kincaid thought, yet they were flirting with their eyes.

"Shall we shoot some pool?" Jess shouted in Kincaid's direction.

Who was he to get in the way of true love—or lust, probably, in this case? "Sure."

An hour later the band played a slow dance. Big Dave and Jess danced together as Kincaid continued to play pool. He didn't mind them dancing, but it was thwarting the goal of his evening out, so it irritated him. They could at least tone it down a little.

When it was his turn to shoot, he scratched, not hitting any ball on the table with his, which was humiliating.

Aggie came up beside him. "You upset about something, Kincaid?"

"My clumsiness," he answered as his opponent took over the table.

"Your date and Big Dave seem kind of cozy," Aggie said.

"It's a free country."

Aggie's hearty laugh broke the sound barriers of the band. People turned and stared.

So much for keeping a low profile, Kincaid thought as Doc tugged Aggie away. Kincaid's efforts to do Dixie a favor were having results he hadn't anticipated, particularly public humiliation.

He plunked the end of his cue on the floor and leaned against it, ignoring the interest of the crowd.

Then he wondered for the twentieth time what Shana was doing on her first night in his house.

* * *

Shana debated whether to be in bed when Kincaid got home, as if she didn't care what time he got in, or to be up watching television, which was what she wanted to do. She didn't have a television of her own. The one at the apartment belonged to Dixie, and Shana had left it for Dylan.

Deciding she was too wound up to go to bed, she popped popcorn and chose a movie from Kincaid's library of DVDs. She didn't know how to start a fire, so she didn't try, but she cozied into the living room sofa with her bowl and a blanket.

Just as the movie started, her cell phone rang.

"Hey, honey, it's Aggie."

"You sound like you're at a ballgame."

"You could call it a game. I'm at the Stompin' Grounds."

Questions popped into Shana's head. She didn't ask even one. "I hope you're having a good time."

"I am. It's also been highly entertaining."

Shana knew Aggie was just drawing out the suspense. "How nice for you. Who'd you go with?"

"Doc Saxon," she answered, sounding distracted. "But that's—"

"You and Doc are dating?"

"No, we're not dating. I corralled him to come with me so I could watch Kincaid."

"Tsk, tsk, Aggie. Now you're spying?"

"Aren't you interested?" Aggie asked, frustrated.

More than you'll ever know. "Should I be? He's my boss. I probably shouldn't know too much about his personal life." Now Shana was having fun, because she knew Aggie would tell her, no matter what she said.

"You live with him! You're going to know everything about his personal life."

"Oh, yeah. I forgot."

Aggie finally laughed. "You're pulling my leg. I get it now. Anyway, it's all been fascinating here."

"In what way?"

"Kincaid brought this woman, kind of pretty, but older than him and looks like a lady who's the boss of something. In charge, you know?"

Did they hold hands? Dance close? Kiss?

"So, this woman, Jess, she starts a flirtation with Big Dave over a game of pool, then they dance, all slathered up against each other, and Kincaid's at the pool table himself, so mad he scratches his next shot. Then as soon as the dance is over, Jess moseys on up to Kincaid and whispers in his ear, and they leave. Not holding hands or anything, either. So, I followed them out to the parking lot."

"Against my pleading," Doc called out in the background. "Nosy woman."

"How else could I find out anything? Anyway," Aggie went on, "they stood out there talking for a minute, then she got in her fancy little blue Mercedes Benz convertible, but she didn't go anywhere. Kincaid got in his truck and took off. Pretty soon, Big Dave comes out and she follows him down the road!"

Shana was stuck between being happy that the date didn't go well and sympathy for Kincaid. No one wanted to be rejected in public.

And he'd done it because she'd made him. Guilt settled around her.

"Have you been dancing with Doc?" Shana asked, not wanting to know if there was more.

After a couple of beats, Aggie said, "He's light on his feet."

"Have you got white-coat syndrome, Aggie?"

"What's that?"

"When your blood pressure rises upon seeing the doctor."

Aggie cackled. "Maybe. It's been a long time since I've had a night out with anyone other than family," she said more seriously.

"Well, you go, girlfriend. Enjoy it. And him."

They ended the call. Shana tried to snuggle in and watch the movie but she found herself waiting for the sound of Kincaid's truck. It was a ten-minute drive from the bar to his house. He must've gone somewhere else, although nothing was open this time of night other than the diner, at least in town.

An hour passed. The movie didn't grab her interest, but she left it running so that if he came home, it would look as if she'd had a perfectly nice evening. Finally the sound of his truck reached her. She tucked her blanket around her a little more and picked up the half-full bowl of popcorn she'd set on the coffee table. It was only ten o'clock, early to be home from a Saturday night date by anyone's measure.

She waited until he came into the house before she paused the movie.

"Hi," she said cheerfully, refraining from asking how his night was.

"Hey." He hung up his jacket on the coatrack, then went to the fireplace. "No fire?" he asked.

"I was never a Boy Scout."

He nodded. "I'll teach you. It's one of the pleasures of this house, I think. What're you watching?"

"The original *Rambo*."

"I wouldn't have guessed that was something you'd choose."

"Your choice of DVDs is action and more action. Anyway, the movie came out when I was a baby. I hadn't seen it."

He patiently got the fire going. The silence in the room seemed loud, a hum of discomfort permeating the space.

"You haven't asked how my evening was," he said, poking at the logs, but it seemed to be just a reason to keep his back to her and his hands busy.

"I didn't want to intrude."

He laughed, a little harshly, she thought.

"As if I don't know that Aggie hasn't already called you," he said. "I saw her lurking in the shadows in the parking lot."

Shana sighed. "I didn't ask her to file a report with me, but—" she shrugged "—you know Aggie."

"I won't do that again, Shana."

"Do what?"

"Take a woman out as a ruse. If I take someone out, it'll be because it's what I want to do. I don't care what people think about us. Tonight wasn't worth it."

"I'm sorry. I truly am. I just didn't want there to be talk about us."

"I know." He sat at the other end of the sofa. "There'll be talk, regardless. All we can do is ignore it."

"And show them it isn't true."

"Right." He stared at the fire. "So, how was your evening?"

"It was nice. Emma and I played and read books. She loved the bath toys you put in her tub for her." The man was killing her with kindness. "Thank you."

"Kids need toys."

"You seem to have spent the week preparing for us to arrive. You gave it a lot of thought."

"I'm a planner," he said.

"I've become one, too."

"I know." He smiled a little. "Maybe we've always butted heads because we're too much alike."

"Maybe." If it had been anyone else, she would've chalked it up to unresolved sexual attraction. But this was Kincaid. She couldn't afford the attraction. "And then there's Aggie and Doc Saxon, who are opposites. That was a surprise to hear they were together."

He eyed her thoughtfully. "I'm pretty sure that was just a ploy so that she had an excuse to take a look at my date."

"Still, isn't it fun to think about? Aggie's been alone a long time. Who knows what might happen?" She passed him the bowl of popcorn. "Want to watch the rest of the movie? There's about fifteen minutes left."

"Sure."

She started the movie again, aware of him at the

other end of the couch, eating popcorn, as if they were an old married couple. He got up once to stoke the fire. When he sat down, he tugged her blanket over her feet, wrapping them up.

She felt as if he'd hugged her.

What might seem to be a small gesture to him mattered a lot to her. He didn't want her to get cold. It'd been so long since anyone had cared like that.

Dangerous thinking, she realized. And she was jumping to conclusions. He'd been kind to Emma, too.

The movie ended.

"Do you have plans for tomorrow?" he asked as he ejected the DVD and put it away.

"I'm going to drive to Sacramento to do a little shopping. I want to personalize Emma's and my rooms a little."

"Want company?"

She couldn't hide her shock. "Why would you do that?"

"I'm thinking you need a new car. You could pick out what you want."

The silence returned, louder than ever. "You're buying me a car?" she asked finally.

"A company car, but yours to use as long as you're working for me."

"Mine will do just fine," she said, standing and bunching up the blanket to take with her, not taking time to fold it.

He stood, too. "Your car is junkyard material."

"It's been getting me to work and back just fine for a year."

"Has it? I heard you borrowed Dixie's car several times."

"She asked me to. She didn't want it to sit idle the whole time they were gone." Which was the truth, but Shana had only borrowed it when she was having trouble with her own car.

Kincaid crossed his arms. "I need you to have a reliable car so I know you'll get to appointments on time. A lot of these jobs are out of town. Some are as far away as Lake Tahoe. We're coming into winter. There'll be rain and snow to contend with."

She was being foolish not to accept his offer. She prided herself on her punctuality and reliability, but more than that, having a decent car to haul Emma around mattered more than anything.

"There's no need to get me a *new* car," she said, giving in but on her own terms. "Used would be fine."

"You can choose the car, but since I'm paying for it, it'll be new because that's my preference. Quit being stubborn."

She was fascinated by how his jaw twitched when he was annoyed. She almost reached out to run her fingers along his skin to soothe him. "You're the boss."

"Yes, I am."

She almost laughed. He thought *she* was stubborn? Ha..

"On that note, I'll say good-night." She climbed the stairs, knowing he was staring after her, probably wondering what she was up to, not arguing back. She figured he'd had enough upset for one night at her expense.

Tomorrow, however, was another day.

Chapter Six

Watching Kincaid negotiate a deal for the car reminded Shana how much of a businessman he was. She usually thought about him in terms of his construction work, taking on a variety of jobs, always working hard physically. But he also hired subcontractors, and priced and bid contracts, which required exceptional estimating skills or he risked losing money. He bought, remodeled and sold houses.

She felt a little wheeled and dealed herself as she drove back to Chance City in her brand-new SUV. He'd said she could pick out what car she wanted, then he'd talked her into something bigger and sturdier.

She'd never owned a new car before. "That's new-car smell," she said to Emma in the backseat.

"Pretty," Emma said.

Shana grinned. She still couldn't believe her luck. She'd kept her nose to the grindstone for a whole year, and it had paid off. No one had even one smidge of gossip about her to spread. Not that it had changed her father's mind. He still didn't want to spend time with her, although he was aware that her mother came to visit.

Shana wondered if they argued about that. Had her mother finally stood up to him about something? She sure hadn't stood up for Shana, which had contributed to her rebelling well beyond the normal teenage amount. Now, when she wanted her parents' forgiveness, she hadn't gotten it, even after a year of good behavior.

Maybe she never would. Maybe she needed to resign herself to that. "I guess it's true that you can't go home again," she said with a sigh. She'd changed too much. Starting anew was her only option. The problem was she was starting new in the same old town.

"Go home," Emma said emphatically.

"We're almost there, peapod. Are you hungry?" They'd eaten lunch at a restaurant near the auto dealership while the SUV was being detailed, but that was several hours and a bed, bath and toy shopping trip ago.

"Mmm."

"That's a yes, I take it?" Shana asked as she took the exit toward home, Kincaid right behind her. "Can you say yes?"

"No!"

Shana waved at people she knew as they drove through the charming downtown. Friends stopped and stared then recognized her and waved back, or gave a thumbs-up or shouted hello. Within ten minutes everyone would know she had a new car, a fancy one with four-wheel drive, a killer sound system, satellite telephone and whatever other luxury features it came with. Since her old car hadn't even had working air conditioning, she would've been happy just with that.

She pulled into the driveway. Kincaid carried their purchases into the house.

"How'd it run?" he asked.

"Terrible." She set Emma down just inside the door. "Like a tank."

"Are you serious?" He didn't shut the door, but stared at the vehicle. "Give me your keys."

"Why?"

"I want to drive it. If I'm going to take it back—"

"I'm kidding, Kincaid. It's smooth and powerful, even going uphill. I had to be really careful to stick to the speed limit."

He gave her a look she couldn't decipher. Tolerant, maybe, of her joke? Then he shut the door and headed upstairs. "I'll put your stuff in your room."

She realized they had the whole evening ahead of them. He hadn't said anything about going out, anyway.

"Mama, eat," Emma said, patting her stomach.

Shana had settled Emma in her high chair with her favorite finger foods when Kincaid returned. He'd been upstairs for about ten minutes.

"I got a call from Tom Orwell," he said. "There's a problem at his house with the kitchen job. Someone broke in and spray painted graffiti on the new cabinets. I'm going to check it out. Dylan's meeting me there."

Emma gave him a serious look as he swiped some grated cheese off her tray. "Kinky no."

He ruffled her hair. "Sorry, Miss Emma. I was hungry."

She went back to eating but eyed him the whole time.

"Kincaid," Shana said before he reached the kitchen door.

He turned just in time to catch the keys she tossed him. "Take it for a test run."

He grinned. "Thanks."

"You own it," she said to herself after he left. She didn't want to start thinking it was hers, since she would have to return it when she left his employ.

She'd just put Emma down for a nap when her cell phone rang. She took a steadying breath when she saw who was calling, then said hello.

"Are you avoiding me?" her mother asked.

"Not on purpose. I've been busy, Mom."

"So I hear. You've got a new place to live. And a fancy new car."

"That's right." Shana made her way down the staircase to sit on the bottom step. "Would you like to come see the house?"

A long pause ensued, then, "When?"

Shana wanted to prove she had nothing to hide, no relationship to keep secret. "Right now, if you want." She took a chance then. "Bring Dad. Kincaid's not here."

"I'll ask him," she said hesitantly. "But you know…"

"I do know, Mom."

"Okay. See you in a few."

Shana raced upstairs to brush her hair and change from her T-shirt to a nice blouse. She filled a kettle to make a pot of peppermint tea, her mother's favorite, then set a few snicker doodle cookies on a small plate.

If only Dixie were here. She'd keep the conversation flowing. She knew how to handle their mother. Shana had made a kind of peace with her mom during the past year, an unspoken agreement that they wouldn't talk about where and how Shana had spent the years she'd been gone. They only briefly discussed what had happened to Emma's father.

Maybe this was the time to open up?

She'd just poured the hot water into the teapot when the doorbell rang. Shana pressed her hands to her stomach as she walked to the front door.

You came alone.

Shana tamped down her disappointment. She wanted her father to see how well she was doing, not just hear it from her mother.

"Hi, Mom!" Shana gave her a big hug, probably surprising her. There'd never been much physical affection in their family. Shana never knew families hugged a lot until she'd gotten to know Aggie McCoy and the rest of her clan well.

"Kincaid's truck is the only one outside," her mother said as a greeting.

"He's driving mine at the moment. Come in."

"Where's Emma?"

Her mother wore her hair in a bun on top of her head,

as usual, hairpins visible here and there. It was her green eyes that all three of her children had inherited. She was sturdy, but fading a little each year, hunching a little, too.

"Emma is napping. I'd just put her down before you called, so there's a chance she'll wake up while you're here."

"This is some house. Like everyone else, I watched it being built. Kincaid's been a customer at the store for a lot of years, orders a lot of his supplies from us." She came inside, taking it all in, much like Shana had her first time. "It's a far cry from where you grew up, isn't it?"

No kidding. "I don't own it. I'm just working here."

"Is that really the truth?" Beatrice Callahan took off her jacket and passed it to Shana, who noticed, not for the first time, how aged her mother's hands looked. She should be retired by now, but until their hardware store found a buyer, her father wouldn't stop working, so her mom was stuck, too. The store had been on the market for over a year without a single offer.

"Yes, Mom. Really. I'm Kincaid's housekeeper, but he's also employed me for other aspects of his work." She gestured toward the sofa. "I made a pot of tea, and I've got cookies."

"You know people are talking, don't you?" Bea asked as she sat.

"It wouldn't be Chance City without the grapevine." Shana smiled as she poured two cups of tea, as if she wasn't worried about the same thing. "It's strictly business, Mom. I won't have to commute to Sacramento anymore, and Kincaid's going to help me get my design business off the ground. He's making it possible for me to have a real future. And what's good for me is good for Emma."

Bea frowned. "I thought those decorating jobs you did were favors. You know, your hobby."

Shana figured everyone else probably thought the same thing. "I got paid for those jobs, Mom. It's what I'd like to do as a career. Maybe I've only had three clients so far, but they were thrilled with my work."

"Don't you need an education for that?"

"I'm sure that would be very helpful, but it's out of the question at the moment. I've been studying a lot on my own, plus I have a knack for it. Everyone says so."

"People do try to be kind…" Her voice trailed off.

Thanks for the vote of confidence, Mom. Shana had vowed long ago to be a different kind of parent than her own. Her daughter would feel supported and approved of.

Shana wanted her to have siblings, too. Without her own brother and sister while growing up, she would've had little family life.

She watched her mother sip her tea and enjoy the cookie and wondered—

"Are you happy, Mom?"

"What kind of question is that?"

"A simple one, I think."

She wrapped her hands around her teacup, as if its warmth could give her strength. "Well, you know, Shana, life is what it is. You work, you eat, you rest. You're a good citizen. You don't expect special treatment from anyone. Eventually you go to your Maker, so you'd better have lived a clean life. I've done all that, so I guess that would make me a happy person. Do I wish your father would retire? Yes. Ever since we rented that RV last year and hit the road, I got a yearning to do more of that before it's too late. He'll be seventy-eight next month, you know."

Shana did know that. Her mother had been forty-three and her father forty-seven when she was born. They'd always been old to her, but especially now. Shana and her siblings had talked about how it had felt to them as if they'd been raised by their grandparents. It wasn't just their age, but their attitude.

"Why won't he give it up?" Shana asked. "What if the store never sells?"

"He'll stay, that's all. Like many men, he's tied to his work. It's who he is."

"But does that mean you have to be, too? Don't you want to take some time for yourself? You could be with Emma more, and with Gavin and Becca's baby when it's born in April." Shana had never had such a personal conversation with her mother before, and she kept waiting for her to either clam up or leave in a huff, but instead she sipped her tea thoughtfully and seemed to ponder the questions.

"Your father and I are a team," she said finally, but Shana thought there was much more to her answer.

"Mama!" Emma called from upstairs. She rarely woke up crying, but *always* woke up demanding.

"I'm coming, peapod," Shana called back. "You'll stay and visit awhile longer, won't you, Mom?"

"A little while, yes."

Shana hurried up the stairs. She stuck her head in Emma's doorway. "Boo!"

Emma giggled, delighted, and raised her hands to be lifted down.

"Diaper change first, baby girl."

"Diappy."

Shana made quick work of it. "Grandma Bea's downstairs waiting to see you."

Emma frowned, as if trying to recall who that was.

Shana wasn't surprised that Emma couldn't remember her grandmother, they spent so little time together. Maybe when her mother finally retired, that would change. In the meantime, Aggie was the one Emma had bonded with the most.

Shana had just reached the bottom stair when Kincaid came through the door. He couldn't have missed seeing her mom's car out front, which meant he'd voluntarily come inside. She gave him a lot of credit for that.

"Kinky," Emma said solemnly to him.

"Hello, Miss Emma," Kincaid said. "Did you have a good nap?"

"All done."

"Hi, Bea," he said. "How're you? Did Malcolm come, too?"

"I'm well, thank you." She sat a little straighter. "Malcolm's at the store, as usual. I'm sorry if I'm intruding, but Shana did invite me."

"You're welcome here anytime. As I told Shana, this is her home, too."

Her mother's back went a little straighter. "But she's your employee."

"A technicality." He looked at Shana. "I came to get my truck. I need tools."

"How bad is the damage at the Orwells'?"

"The cabinets will need a lot of sanding, but it won't be noticeable when we're done. Dylan needs to bulk up his muscles, anyway." He grinned.

"I could bring you both dinner later on, if you like."

He went still and silent for a minute, as if he didn't know what to say. "That'd be great, thanks. Maybe at six?"

"Okay. I could sand tomorrow, too, if you have another job to get to."

"We'll see how it goes. Thanks for offering. Bea, please do come back. Tell Malcolm to come, too."

Then he was gone. Zoom in, zoom out.

"Kinky!" Emma shouted, as if upset at his leaving.

"Really, Shana, can't you teach her to say his real name? That's embarrassing."

"I'm sure in time she will. Would you like more tea?"

"No, thank you. I think I'll run along."

"But Emma just got up."

"Your father is expecting me." She stood. "I've always liked Kincaid. He's respectful and serious, but I don't like that you've moved in here, no matter what you say about it just being a job. It's not right. There'll be talk."

"I've survived worse."

"What's that supposed to mean?"

"I mean I'm an unwed mother. People talk. It doesn't matter to me."

"Well, thank you so much for taking your father and me into consideration."

"I'm sorry, Mom. I do take you into consideration. I do care." She picked up Emma. "Come on, baby girl. Let's walk Grandma to her car."

"So there's your new car," her mother said as they went down the steps to the driveway. "Pretty spiffy shade of blue."

"I like it."

"I imagine you do." She started to climb into her ten-year-old hatchback without hugging either Shana or Emma goodbye, but Shana was having none of that. She handed Emma to her mother for a hug, which brought a smile to her face finally. Then Shana gave her a big hug, too.

"Bye-bye," Emma said, waving.

"Bye-bye, Emma. Bye-bye." Bea glanced at Shana. "She looks like you did when you were that age."

"My hair was curly?" It'd been stick straight for as long as she could remember.

"Until kindergarten, I think. I'll look for some pictures for you." She rolled up her window and took off.

Shana hugged Emma tight and kissed her forehead. "Shall we go see what we can fix for Kincaid and Dylan for dinner?"

Emma clapped her hands and giggled. "No!"

Shana laughed. "Yes!"

"No."

"Okay. We'll stay home."

"No! Dilly." She pouted.

"Then you need to say yes."

There was a momentary battle of wills, then Emma said, "Yessss."

"See? That wasn't so hard." They went into the house and straight to the kitchen. Emma played on the floor in the breakfast nook, pulling out toys from a basket, as Shana made a big pot of chili and a pan of cornbread.

A little before six o'clock they loaded the car and drove to the Orwell house. Emma raced ahead as Shana carried the pot then went back for everything else.

"How long did your mother stay?" Kincaid asked a few minutes later as they sat at the kitchen table, the Orwell family having gone out to eat. Fortunately the family owned a high chair, and Dylan was keeping Emma occupied.

"Mom left shortly after you did."

"I hesitated when I got there. I didn't know whether to just come back later or to see if you needed rescuing." He grinned, as if making a joke.

"Thank you." She meant it. His thoughtfulness continued to catch her off guard.

Kincaid's expression changed. "Are things that bad between you?"

"They're improving. It's just been a slow process."

"I knew you weren't real close, but that's all."

Shana didn't want to talk about it in front of Dylan, but then Dylan said, "I'm not close to my dad, either. Actually, he's my foster dad, but I never think about him that way. It kind of hurt that I was with him and my foster mom since I was six, but he never wanted to adopt me. Mom would've." He angled his head at Kincaid. "He taught me how to let go of that, said that people usually do the best they can, and we shouldn't live our lives angry about something we can't change. Didn't think I was paying attention, did you?" Dylan asked Kincaid, grinning.

Shana wondered about Kincaid's past now in a way she hadn't before. Everyone knew he'd emancipated himself and moved here but not why. If he really had let go of a painful past, she admired him for that, but maybe he'd told Dylan to do what he, Kincaid, hadn't been able to. Lots of people were good at advising others how to do something they hadn't been able to do themselves.

Shana took Emma home, gave her a bath and put her to bed, then she hauled a load of laundry downstairs. She loaded the washer, turned the dial then felt the sting of tears in her eyes and throat as she realized it was the first time in years she hadn't had to trek to a coin-operated laundry.

She stood staring at the washer as it filled with water. Sometimes it was the little things in life that made the difference, in this case not having to entertain Emma while she did the laundry, which took a couple of hours, generally. She could do one load at a time as her baby girl slept. She didn't have to stockpile quarters. She could take things out of the dryer and hang them right away in the closet, preventing the wrinkles that came with putting them in the car and transporting them.

Suddenly the wonderful change in her life overwhelmed her. She'd been fighting letting herself enjoy it, not wanting to get too comfortable. It always seemed that whenever she found comfort, it got snatched away.

But in this house she slept in a big, soft bed, and her daughter had a bright, airy bedroom, and a yard with a play structure, and a mother who wasn't struggling and stressed every second of every day.

And Shana wasn't a charity case. Kincaid had hired her because he needed her skills. He'd said so, more than once. She was truly earning her own way.

Scalding hot tears of joy rolled down her cheeks. She hunched over and let them come. She had a right to be happy. Deserved to be happy. She'd been unhappy for so very long.

"What's wrong?"

Kincaid had stepped into the laundry room, startling her. She hadn't heard his truck pull up outside.

She could barely speak, but she couldn't let him worry, either. "Nothing. I'm happy. I've never felt safer in my life. Thank you so much."

They stared at each other for a few seconds, then somehow his arms came around her and she felt secure and good and warm. And he felt strong and solid and reliable. Which made her cry harder, releasing tears dammed up for years.

She felt him stroke her hair and heard his whispered, "It's okay. It's okay," in her ear, and she pushed herself even closer, relishing the moment of comfort. His arms locked around her then. She didn't want to be anywhere but there, right there.

Amazingly he didn't end the embrace, as if knowing

her mental health depended on this moment, so finally she moved back. She made eye contact, saw tenderness in his eyes, and understanding. He grabbed a towel off the dryer and passed it to her. She didn't know what to say, and he wasn't saying anything at all.

Finally she tried to smile. "I guess I just blew my tough-as-nails reputation with you, huh?"

He framed her face with his hands, and then he kissed her. His lips felt cool against hers as he lingered, not deepening the kiss but fully arousing her, anyway.

Yes, she thought, twining her arms around his neck. *Oh, yes....*

Then, "No." She pulled away, shaking her head, her hands flattened on his sturdy chest. She yanked them back, closed them into fists, then finally looked at him. He was serious more often than not, but now he looked grim.

"Why did you do that?" she asked.

"I wanted to," he said as if it was obvious.

His answer jarred her. It seemed so...unKincaid-like. "Well, you can't do it again."

"Why not?"

Confounded herself, she plunked her fists on her hips. "Because we're supposed to have a professional relationship."

"But I liked it." He leaned forward. "You seemed to like it, too."

"That has nothing to do with anything."

He smiled slightly. "Doesn't it? Surprised the hell out of me, frankly, Shana, but there you have it. And you did stop crying."

"That's not why you kissed me."

"Isn't it? Why, then?"

"It's the proximity. I knew it was going to be a problem."

"If you already knew you were attracted to me, why did you say yes to the job?"

"I didn't know! I thought I didn't like you." She was utterly confused.

"I felt the same. Looks like we were wrong."

Oh, he was being so cool, so calm, so…accepting of what was now a huge problem for them.

She couldn't deal with it until she thought about it some more, so she threw up her hands and walked away. "I'm going to bed."

"At nine o'clock?"

She reached the staircase and started up.

"Sweet dreams, Shana."

That did it. He was laughing at her. She turned around and marched back to him, grabbed his head and pulled him down for an all-out-assault kiss, a blistering, thorough melding of mouths and tongues. He didn't waste any time catching up, either, his hands gliding down to cup her rear and pull her against him.

He groaned and came at her from a different angle. She moaned and went up on tiptoe. His mouth was hot and demanding. She took what he offered and gave him more back. Everything she'd yearned for these past two years poured from her and into him. She might have kept going, too, except he slid his hands up her sides, his fingertips grazing her breasts. It was like turning a light switch on in her head. *Wake up, you fool! Wake the heck up!*

She wrenched herself away and made herself smile, seemingly unruffled. "Sweet dreams to you, too, Kincaid."

And with that, she turned and went back up the stairs, willing herself not to look back.

Chapter Seven

The scent of bacon cooking greeted Kincaid when he opened his bedroom door the next morning. He'd overslept after a long night of fantasy-filled, high-passion dreams that had left his sheets tangled and his heart racing. He couldn't say he regretted kissing her last night, but he recognized that their relationship was bound to change now.

At some point during the night he'd decided it'd been coming for a long time. They'd been edgy around each other for a reason, but he'd finally figured out it wasn't because they disliked each other. On the surface it might look like that, but it wasn't true. It *was* tension—just not the kind they'd thought all along.

He'd known that sharing the same house wouldn't

be easy, but he hadn't expected things to change so quickly.

Kincaid went downstairs. The sounds of Emma babbling should have relaxed him, since he wouldn't be alone with Shana. All he had to do was ignore what happened last night, hope that she would also join in the pretense and then make his escape to work.

Except…she needed to come with him this morning.

"Good morning," Shana said from the stove, sort of glancing his way as he came into the kitchen. "Coffee's ready."

"Thanks." He got a mug from the cupboard and poured himself a cup, wishing Emma hadn't stopped babbling. She'd gone silent as she watched his every move, her expression serious, her eyes the same vivid green as Shana's.

Truth be known, Emma terrified him more than any adult ever had. Shana might be her mother, but he'd assumed responsibility now, too. He'd really had no idea what he was getting himself into.

"Good morning, Miss Emma," he said.

She stabbed some scrambled eggs with her tiny blunt fork but the eggs fell off, so she grabbed them with her fist and stuffed them in her mouth, flattening her hand against her lips so that the eggs wouldn't fall out.

"Say good morning to Kincaid, Emma," Shana said as she filled two plates with bacon, eggs and toast.

Emma gave him that belligerent look she'd perfected, the one that usually made him want to laugh. He figured he shouldn't encourage her. He wished he knew more about what to do with her. Some people were naturals with kids, but he really hadn't been around many, especially one this young.

"Get it while it's hot," Shana said, setting their plates on the counter.

"It all looks great, thanks." He waited for her to sit, too, before he started, trying to remember the last time someone had fixed him breakfast. Usually he ate a bowl of cereal or stopped by the Lode. Homemade was a rare treat.

They ate in silence, Emma making enough noise for all of them, but he had no idea what she was saying. Every so often a word came through clearly, but the gist of her conversation was lost on him.

"Did you sleep okay?" he finally asked Shana.

She stopped eating. "What's that supposed to mean?"

Uh-oh. It sounded as if she'd had a worse night than he had. "I didn't mean anything by it, Shana. I was being polite. We live together. Being cordial would seem preferable."

"We don't live together." She picked up her empty plate and carried it to the sink. "I work for you. It happens to involve my living in your house, but we don't live together."

"I stand corrected." He passed his empty plate to her. She almost snatched it out of his hands. "Are you expecting an apology from me for last night?"

"No." She kept her back to him as she rinsed the dishes and put them in the dishwasher.

"Okay. Then what *can* I do to make you feel at

ease?" Because he couldn't live with all this tension in his home, his refuge.

"Done?" she asked Emma.

"All done." She picked up her bowl and gave it to Shana, who scooped up the remnants from the tray before she returned to the sink.

"I apologize, okay?" Shana said, her tight voice aimed at the tiled wall behind the sink. "We got carried away last night. I think it caught both of us off guard—at least it did me. But that's the end of it."

"It?" He liked that she was riled up and confused. So was he. And he liked it for himself, too.

She sighed and turned around, finally looking him in the eye. "The kissing. The enticing."

"Oh, *that* it." Enticing? An interesting word choice. "It was just a fluke, Shana. We probably had to get it out of our systems."

She eyed him as warily as Emma had earlier. "Is it out of your system?"

Not even close. "Well…I could lie to you, but we agreed to be honest. That said, I am an adult. I don't pursue if I'm not wanted." He didn't want to continue the discussion. "Is Aggie watching Emma today?"

"Aggie!" Emma shouted as Shana cleaned her up.

"Yes. She can keep her all day, if necessary."

"Good. I'm not sure how long everything will take. You can meet me at the Orwell house after you've dropped her off."

"All right."

Damn, she was pretty. Soft and feminine in jeans and a plaid shirt she'd probably chosen because she didn't think it was sexy, but it was, even with all but the top button fastened so that there was no danger of any cleavage showing. He'd felt just the sides of her breasts last night before she pulled away, his thumbs pressing into her flesh momentarily, enough to make him want more.

Shana started to walk past him with Emma in her arms. He stopped her, putting a hand on her shoulder briefly.

"Are we okay?" he asked.

"We have to be," she said.

He got it. This job meant everything to her, as did her reputation. She was straddling a line between what she needed and what she wanted. So was he. They were young, single and healthy, and there was a previously unacknowledged attraction between them. Factor in that they lived in the same house, and it got really complicated.

He tapped Emma's nose and smiled at her, getting a smile in return finally, albeit a fleeting one, as if she couldn't help herself. It pleased him enormously.

"I'll see you later, Miss Emma."

He had to stop himself from kissing Shana goodbye, which seemed like the most natural thing to do.

"Do you want me to make lunches for you and Dylan?" she asked.

"Thanks, but we'll manage on our own."

"I don't mind."

"We never know what time we're going to break for lunch, and sometimes we're not even working at the same site. If you'll do breakfast and dinner, at least most of the time, that works for me. We'll go out occasionally, too." He walked across the room, grabbed his work vest from the coatrack. "I'll see you in a bit?"

"Twenty minutes or so."

"Good." He left. The crisp December air energized him. He had a big garage, but he rarely used it, preferring to have his truck ready to go in an instant. Shana's SUV was parked in it. It would be easier for her to get Emma in and out in bad weather and go right into the kitchen. He liked that Emma wouldn't have to walk through dirt to get into the house—and that Shana wouldn't have to carry her.

You're thinking like a family man.

No, just a practical man, he decided, which was a good thing.

"Looks like you survived your first weekend okay," Aggie said to Shana as Emma raced by her into the living room and the big toy box there.

"Of course we did. It was easy." *Right. Sure it was.*

"I heard his date's car was still at Big Dave's house until Sunday morning."

"Really? And was Doc's car here until Sunday morning, too?"

"Of course not," she said indignantly, then she grinned like a girl. "I know this town better. He would have to leave his car at home and walk over."

"Aggie McCoy," Shana said in pretend shock.

She shrugged. "It didn't happen, but I do know how to handle that kind of situation."

"Did you enjoy yourself?"

"I did."

"Will you go out with him again?"

Her eyes sparkling, she nodded. "He already asked. Now, don't go telling stories about us, okay? We're going to try to keep it on the down low."

"Good luck with that. Emma, come give me a hug, please. I need to get to work."

"Bye-bye, Mama. Bye-bye," she said as Shana hugged her close.

"I don't have any idea what time I'll be through," Shana said to Aggie. "I'll keep in touch."

A few minutes later she pulled up at the Orwell house. She was excited about starting work. No two days would be the same, but that was good. She was up to the challenge.

"Morning, Shana," Dylan said as she stepped into the kitchen. They were still sanding the cabinet faces, but the graffiti was all but gone.

"Everything okay with Aggie?" Kincaid asked.

Shana decided to let him hear the rumors about his date staying over with Big Dave from someone else. It would seem like she was rubbing it in or...*cared* or something. "Aggie's good. Emma adores her, so it's never an issue to leave her there. Now, what can I do?"

"I need you to pick up stain for the cabinets. We're just about ready for that step." He caught her gaze, his expression bland. "I called your dad. He's got it in stock."

Did Kincaid know how little she and her father communicated? "Okay," she said, but feeling far from it.

"After that, I'll take you to one of my rentals," he

said. "The tenant just moved out, so it needs cleaning, at least. We'll assess what else needs to be done,
and you can decide how much you want to tackle, and
what's beyond your ability."

She was confident in the life skills she'd acquired
along the way. "Sounds good," she said. She wasn't as
confident about going to her father's store. So far, she'd
avoided her father's domain since she'd been back.

To settle her nerves—and maybe even to stall a
little—Shana walked the three blocks to the hardware store, which was a general term for the small-
town business. They didn't stock just tools and parts
but also small appliances, assorted household supplies,
paint and some lumber, and they could special order
anything. Her mom would be there, running the cash
register, doing the books, but she didn't otherwise work
with the customers.

Did her daughter qualify as a customer? Shana wondered.

Her heart raced as she opened the door and stepped
inside, the door chime jarring but the familiar smell
oddly comforting, even with all the bad memories that
came with it.

It shook her up more than she'd expected. Her
knees wobbled, her pulse pounded in her ears and she
couldn't take a normal breath. She'd expected to be
doing manual labor today, so she wore sturdy clothes
and boots. Now she tugged her sweatshirt closer to her
body, making it her armor.

She didn't see her mother, but her father was talking
to Bruno Manning, another local contractor. Dixie had

hired and fired the man before hiring Kincaid instead to build Respite. They'd worked closely together. Kincaid had fallen for Dixie—

"Why, hello, Shana," her mother said, having come up to her while Shana was lost in thought.

Shana hugged her, once again startling her. Over her mother's shoulder she said, "Hi, Dad."

He gave her a nod, then he angled away, returning to his conversation. He looked skinny to the point of boniness. Dixie had been worried about his health for a while now, but he wasn't about to slow down. Shana only worried that her mother's health would suffer because of his stubbornness.

"What brings you here?" her mother asked.

"Kincaid called in an order for some stain. I'm the gofer. Dad knows about it," she managed to say, feeling light-headed.

Her father hitched a thumb toward the counter, where a quart of stain sat.

"Kincaid has a running account." Bea handed her the can.

"I need to pick up a few things for myself," she said, setting the can on the counter again. She wandered from aisle to aisle, picking up small items. Her mother didn't accompany her. Her father continued his conversation with Bruno, who kept moving toward the door, then finally said, "I gotta run," and took off.

They were alone—mother, father and somewhat estranged daughter. Shana took a settling breath and walked up to the counter, placing a box of paper clips, a kite and a wire whisk next to the can of stain. By the time she turned around, her father had disappeared.

"I'm sorry," her mother whispered. "Why didn't Kincaid come?"

"He's busy." She needed to get out. This hadn't gone well at all. "Maybe you can start an account for me, too, Mom," she said gathering all the items and leaving, not wanting to hang around another second.

She didn't know where to go. She needed a few minutes alone. If her father hadn't welcomed her home by now, would he ever? He'd never spoken much to her, probably because they'd always butted heads, and they'd both ended up frustrated. Some things never changed.

She headed to the creek. This time of year, it ran at a trickle. The dank, mossy smell took her back to childhood and the many times she'd escaped to spend hours there, skipping rocks, hiking and collecting leaves. Dixie and Gavin had been the social ones in the family, always hanging out with friends. Shana did interact with her siblings some but mostly had kept to herself. She'd always done better one on one.

Kincaid would undoubtedly be angry at her for not showing up with the stain right away, but if she didn't take some time for herself, she wouldn't be fit to work at all.

"Shana!"

She bent her head at the sound of Kincaid's voice. *Not yet. Please, not yet.*

She didn't answer him, but he'd spotted her and was coming down the slope, leaves crackling under his boots, and then he was standing above her as she sat on a low rock, her knees pulled up.

He crouched. "Are you all right?"

She shook her head.

He cupped her shoulder. "Your mom called me."

"How did you know I'd be *here?*"

"I tried to think like you."

She sort of laughed. "That must've been a challenge." She hated that he was once again seeing her not being her usual strong self, but she couldn't muster up enough strength to get up yet.

"What happened?"

"Same old, same old."

"He didn't talk to you?"

"How can I get him to forgive me if he won't speak to me? Won't even listen to me for a minute? What kind of man does that to his own child?" She pressed a hand to her mouth as tears burned her eyes.

"What kind of man beats his wife and son *for their own good?*" Kincaid asked in return. "I don't know the answers to those questions. I wish I did."

"Your father?" she asked, horrified.

He nodded.

"Oh." Her heart ached for him. "Oh, I'm so sorry."

"I let it go a long time ago."

Had he? His jaw was like granite, his skin taut, as if he was in pain.

"We're a pair, aren't we?" she asked, stroking his face as if she could soothe the past away. But hearing his story put her relationship with her father into perspective. It could have been a whole lot worse.

"Seems like it."

She pressed her lips gently to his. He returned the kiss with tenderness of his own, warming her, making her feel safe, not turning it into anything like last night's kiss.

"Thank you," she said against his mouth.

"Likewise." He stood, offering her a hand up, then gathered her purchases, giving them a curious look.

She smiled for the first time since she'd walked into the hardware store. It was an odd combination of items. "Do you know how to fly a kite? I thought Emma would like to watch."

"It's been a long time, but I think I can manage it. There's enough open space in the park. Just need some wind." He took her hand and helped her up the banking as she slipped and slid on the blanket of leaves.

She didn't want to let go of him when they reached the top, but he took care of that, dropping her hand right away—which was a good thing, since her sister-in-law, Becca, came driving down the road.

She pulled over. "Everything okay?" she asked.

"Fine," Shana said. "How are you?"

She laid a hand over her rounded belly. "I hit the halfway point in my pregnancy today. No morning sickness. Lots of energy. I feel good. Um, we heard you'd moved in with Kincaid. Gavin and I were going to call you to invite you both to dinner—"

"We're not a couple," they said at the same time. They looked at each other and laughed. "I'm working for him," she said for what seemed like the fiftieth time in a few days.

"Doesn't mean you can't come to dinner together. We like both of you."

"We'll see," Kincaid said. "For now, we've got to get back to work."

She was glad he'd come looking for her, grateful he'd figured out where she'd gone. It would've taken her a whole lot longer to right herself had she been left alone.

Left alone.

She considered the words. She hadn't been left alone but had retreated on her own, as she always had. She never went to anyone for help, always ran away and dealt with it herself. Alone.

Except for the one time she'd broken down with Aggie....

And that hadn't turned out so bad. Not bad at all. There was much more to Kincaid than she'd imagined.

Chapter Eight

"How's apartment living?" Kincaid asked Dylan as they stowed the tools in Kincaid's truck at the end of the workday. They'd accomplished a lot, were only a half day behind schedule. Kincaid figured they'd be caught up by Friday.

"It's kinda weird," Dylan said.

"In what way?"

"I don't know what I expected, because I've never lived on my own before. I guess I just haven't figured out what to do with my time yet."

"You lived alone for months when you were homeless."

"That was different. I only focused on survival. This is all so…comfortable. And quiet."

"Time to branch out and make some friends your own age. Not necessarily girls," Kincaid added.

"Spoilsport." He shrugged. "I'm not ready for that, anyway," he admitted. "Not one on one. But how do I meet guys my age? I didn't go to high school here, so I don't have that connection."

"I'd talk to Aggie. Or even Honey at the Lode." His truck was loaded. "I'm going to swing over and see how Shana's doing. Want to come along?"

"Not unless you need me to. I'd like to go talk to Aggie, get started on a social life."

"I'm pretty sure she has some grandsons about your age," Kincaid said before he got into the truck and took off. The rental property where Shana was working was only about five blocks away—not far enough to give him much thinking time.

The tender moment they'd shared earlier in the day hadn't left his mind, but even after all these hours, he didn't know what to say to her. He hadn't opened up like that with anyone in town, hadn't even hinted at his past, yet he'd told her the worst of it.

Kincaid pulled up behind her car at the rental house. He shoved his hands through his hair, unexpected nerves hitting him. He worried now that she would treat him differently. He didn't want that. He'd made his place in the world by carefully constructing a life for himself, step by step. If anything broke that down, he didn't know what he'd do.

Which is why he should keep his distance from her. He'd been honest last night when he'd told her he'd kissed her because he'd wanted to, which wasn't just an honest statement but an understatement. He wasn't proud of himself for giving in to the temptation of her, but he didn't regret it, either.

"Over and done," he muttered as he climbed out of the truck. So, they knew more about each other now. They were going to share space, after all. Knowing each other well could only help.

Kincaid knocked on the front door then went inside. He called her name but didn't get an answer as he walked through the space. She'd not just cleaned but painted the two bedrooms. The kitchen and bathroom sparkled. She'd pulled down the dining room wallpaper, a garish floral print the previous tenant had put up.

He found Shana's checklist on the fireplace mantel. Only a couple of items weren't checked off. She must not have stopped for lunch, unless she'd combined it with a trip to his storehouse for wall paint.

He spotted her then, raking the backyard. She stopped, stared at her right hand, then shook it before picking up the rake again, and he knew she had to be nursing a blister, probably several.

Kincaid opened the slider and stepped outside, not stopping until he reached her. He grabbed her right hand to look at it, then just as abruptly let go. "The yard wasn't on your task list. And don't you own gloves?"

"I—"

"Wash your hands. I'll get my first-aid kit." He stalked off.

He found her at the kitchen sink when he returned. She kept her back to him.

"Don't treat me like a child," she said with amazing

calmness. "They're just red spots, not open sores, you know."

"A little bit more raking would've changed that."

"I was about to stop."

"Why are you so damned stubborn?" He'd never met a woman so obstinate.

"Because riling you up is entertaining." She flashed him a smile. "And being easygoing is boring."

He hesitated. "I guess I overreacted."

"You think?"

"I've been wound a little tight all day," he admitted.

She dried her hands and leaned against the kitchen counter. "I won't tell anyone what you shared with me."

"It's not that. It just opened up some old wounds, you know?"

She nodded. "This is a cute house," she said.

He looked around, grateful she'd changed the subject. "It's the first one I bought, so there's a lot of sentimentality associated with it. I've purchased many others that I fixed up and sold, but I lived in this one for years. Couldn't make myself give it up."

"Would you consider selling it to me?" she asked.

That caught him off guard. "Why?"

"You said it yourself. In a couple of years, I'll have enough for a down payment. This is a perfect size for Emma and me. It hardly needs anything done to it, just decorating."

He didn't answer her question, even though all he had to do was say maybe. Two years was a long time, he thought. "I noticed you painted the bedrooms."

Her mouth tightened as if perturbed he hadn't answered her. "It was easier than washing them, frankly. The trim was in good shape, so I only needed to roll the walls."

"You put in more than a day's work. How about if we go out to dinner?"

"I fixed a pot roast in the slow cooker this morning, so it'll be ready when we get home. I wouldn't mind stopping at Joe's Christmas tree farm, though, and choosing a tree before all the good ones are gone. Maybe I could pick up Emma first so she could be part of it?"

"We can do that."

"We'll probably have to drive to Grass Valley this weekend to buy a stand and some decorations," she said.

"The hardware store has stands and lights. I saw them."

"And your point is?" She shoved away from the counter and went to where her toolbox sat on the floor, straightening the tools to close the lid. "I changed two light switches and fixed a leak in the bathroom sink. I also cleaned out the P-trap under the kitchen sink. Your new tenants will start with clear pipes, anyway."

"I knew when I hired you that you had your own toolbox, but I had no idea just how handy you are." He set a hand on her shoulder. "We'll go to your parents' store together, Shana. The more he sees you, the more he'll get used to the idea. At some point, things have to change. Although, frankly, I don't know why you have to be the one making all the effort."

"I appreciate what you're trying to do," she said,

shrugging off his hand. "But I'm not up for two cold-shoulder treatments in one day. Maybe tomorrow."

He knew when to back off. "All right. I'll lock up here. You go ahead and get Emma. I'll meet you at the tree farm."

"Thank you." She spoke the words clearly, her head up, then she left.

Damn but he admired her.

He had a few minutes to kill, so he went to the backyard and finished picking up the leaves. By the time he got to the tree farm, Shana and Emma were already there. Overhead lights illuminated the lot. Shana was chasing a giggling Emma up the row right toward him.

The rosy-cheeked little girl came to an abrupt stop a few feet away. She gave him that serious look he'd come to expect. She was wearing a knit cap, her blond hair spilling out below it in wispy curls, halolike.

"Are you having fun?" he asked, crouching to her level.

"No!"

He saw Shana roll her eyes, but he'd come to enjoy Emma's insistent nos.

"Aggie was feeding Dylan dinner when I got there," Shana said. "His timing was perfect for a home-cooked meal."

"Dilly!" Emma said, clapping.

"We should probably invite him to dinner now and then," Kincaid said. "I figure he's on a straight pizza-and-burgers diet."

"Anytime. Emma and I found a tree we'd like you to

see." She held out her hand toward her daughter. "Let's go see the big tree again."

"No." She sat down with a plop. "Home. Eat."

"We'll go home right after we get a tree, I promise."

Emma shook her head back and forth.

"Want to ride on my shoulders?" Kincaid asked.

She contemplated the words. He wasn't sure if she understood what he meant. Her gaze held his for long seconds, then she stood and put her hands up to him. Swallowing the lump in his throat, he lifted her onto his shoulders. He hadn't realized how much he'd wanted her acceptance.

"Mama! Look!"

He caught Shana's gaze. She stared back at him, looking serious, before she answered her daughter. "Isn't that fun, peapod?"

"No!"

Shana groaned. "We worked on this. You know how to say yes."

"No!"

"I guess Kincaid has to put you down, if you're not having fun."

Emma frowned then said, "Kinky. Fun."

Four shoppers and two employees laughed nearby, including Aggie's granddaughter. "Kinky fun, huh?" Posey asked.

One of the shoppers, George Baldwin, said, "We've always wondered what went on in that big ol' house of yours, Kincaid." He eyed Shana then, but didn't make a comment to her directly, then he winked, not a playful one, either.

She eyed his toupee. She was about to make a comment about the wind when Kincaid grabbed a saw from Posey, and shoved it at Shana, propelling her forward.

"Where's this perfect tree you found?" Kincaid asked. He felt Emma grab his hair to hold on.

"Are you crazy?" he asked Shana, low and harsh. "You wanted to stay below the radar yet you were just about to insult the man most likely to start a pool."

She looked over her shoulder. "He annoyed me."

"You annoy me, but I don't embarrass you in public." He could see she was upset, but she was so used to digging in her heels, he didn't know how to get her to see her mistake.

"There's the tree," she said, pointing it out, looking past him to where George still stood, gesturing to a gathering crowd who craned their necks to look toward Shana, Emma and Kincaid. "Do you think he's talking about me?" Shana asked.

"Us, probably." He almost groaned. It had taken even less time than he'd imagined to get everyone's attention focused on them. This entire situation wasn't working out the way he'd hoped. His original goal was to do Dixie a favor, not kiss Shana—more than once—and definitely not have fantasies about her in bed. And now the townspeople had gotten involved.

Well, there was nothing he could do about it except wait for it to blow over.

He eyed the tree, decided it looked pretty good, then he reached up to lift Emma to the ground.

She gripped his head. "No down. No."

"I can't cut the tree while you're on my shoulders, Miss Emma."

"C'mon, baby girl," Shana said, coaxing her.

"No!"

Everyone looked at them. Shana's face flushed. "I already messed up once," she said quietly. "And I don't want to add to it, but I also can't let Emma get away with trying to run the show."

"There's no reasoning with her?"

Shana made Emma look at her. "If you don't let me take you from Kincaid's shoulders, we'll just have to go home without a tree."

"Home."

"It's really an empty threat," she said quietly to Kincaid. "She doesn't understand where the tree is going and what's going to be done to it. What would you do?"

"It seems to me that either way, she's getting what she wants. She doesn't want to get down. She does want to go home."

Shana sighed. "I try to be consistent, so I guess we leave. The threat's been made. I just don't get it. She's usually so well behaved," Shana said apologetically as they walked to the car. "Imagine what she's going to be like as a teenager."

Kincaid laughed, once again drawing the attention of the curious onlookers.

"This is probably payback for what I put my parents through," Shana said. "What goes around, comes around, as they say. Except I'm a hands-on mom, you know? A loving mom. I give her all the attention I didn't get."

"Maybe you're overthinking this," Kincaid said as they reached her car. "She's had a big change in her life. Maybe it's that simple."

A few beats passed. "That makes sense."

"Sometimes I do, you know." He could see she had a comeback but was restraining herself. Because they were being watched by a small crowd? "I'll cut the tree and bring it home."

"I'm really sorry she won't get to be part of that fun."

"Kinky. Fun!"

Kincaid and Shana looked at each other. He asked a question with his eyes. She got it.

"All right, Emma," she said. "Here's your choice. We can have fun with Kincaid or we can go home."

"Kinky. Fun."

"Okay. You have to let me hold you."

Emma raised her arms then settled against her mother, tucking her head in that way she had. She smiled at Kincaid, not an I-got-my-way smile but a sweet one. It melted his heart.

Everything went smoothly after that. The tree was cut down and loaded into his truck without fanfare. He followed Shana and Emma home, pleased he'd insisted on the sturdy new SUV with its brand-new tires as the rain started to fall.

He wondered what the public repercussions of the outing were going to be.

And how long it would be until they found out.

Chapter Nine

"I've never been away from her overnight," Shana said to her brother and sister-in-law. Kincaid had a dinner meeting with a client, leaving Shana at loose ends, so she'd gone to visit Gavin and Becca.

"We want to get some practice in," Becca said, patting her belly. "Besides, wouldn't you like a whole night to yourself?"

"I can't imagine what I would do."

Gavin was on the floor playing train with Emma. "You and Kincaid could—"

"We are not a couple. Honestly, I'm so sick of defending my strictly business relationship with him, Gavin. I was hired. I'm doing a job."

Three days had passed since the Christmas tree farm

fiasco. If there was a pool going, Shana hadn't gotten wind of it.

Gavin flashed a grin at his wife. "That's what we all said. Look at Becca and me. And her brother Eric and Marcy. And all three of the Falcon brothers. It started so innocently...."

She wanted to deny it, but she couldn't. He was right. It had started innocently enough then had escalated. They'd done a good job these past few days, however, of maintaining their distance, except that it had made her more short-tempered and Kincaid oddly quieter.

"Your Christmas tree is gorgeous," Shana said, taking the conversation down a different path.

"Pretty," Emma said, her eyes wide.

"I think everyone in town has already brought us an ornament," Gavin said. "Even those who don't have appointments drop by the practice and leave a decoration and some kind of edible gift, even turkeys and hams. Becca and I decided to put on a Christmas Eve dinner for those in need. Aggie and Doc are co-chairing. We'll need lots of volunteers with the set-up, cleanup and food prep."

"I'll help. I'm sure Kincaid will, too. I hope Dixie and Joe will be home by then." Shana smiled as Emma crawled onto Gavin's back as if he were a horse. He bucked a little and she shrieked a laugh, grabbing his shirt to steady herself, saying, "More, Uncky. More."

"We were already counting on you," Becca said with a knowing smile. "Eric and Marcy have volunteered. It's right up Marcy's party-planning alley, so we're letting her figure out the food plan. We'll have it fairly early, before Christmas Eve services. Do you think it'll snow?"

"It's happened before, but it's rare in December," Gavin said. "Has to be a pretty big, cold storm to come down to the 2500-foot level. So, how about it, Shana? Can we keep your girl overnight on Saturday?"

"We can give it a try. She's never spent the night anywhere without me, so I'm not sure how she'll do."

"Well, you can't stay home just in case, okay?" Becca said. "Grab a girlfriend and head to Sacramento. I can give you the names of a few places where you can kick up your heels. If Emma cries, we'll figure out how to soothe her. She's been around us enough to know us. Go have fun."

Grab a girlfriend. Shana turned that idea over in her head. It hadn't occurred to her before, but she really didn't have a girlfriend. She had lots of friends, but not one single-and-footloose friend she could include in a night on the town. She was closest to Dixie, who now was halfway around the world—and married. Even when she did return to town, she wasn't going to be available in the way she was before.

Shana picked at a piece on lint on the sofa. So, what could she do by herself? She could drive to Grass Valley or Nevada City for the evening, maybe go to the movies. Big deal. Hardly worth the trip. She could go to the Stompin' Grounds, something she had never done and been curious about. But alone? How could she do that?

She couldn't invite Kincaid to go with her, but maybe Aggie would be available? She'd offered a few times in the past to keep Emma overnight—unlike her parents. Aggie would like that Shana was getting out.

"Have you seen Mom and Dad lately?" Shana asked.

"Not Dad," Gavin said as Emma pulled his hair and giggled. "Mom brought by some baby pictures of mine yesterday."

So, her mother had gone through their baby pictures, after all. Shana looked forward to seeing her own. "Are they handy?"

She ended up staying for dinner, figuring the more time Emma spent with her aunt and uncle, the easier it would be on Saturday.

Or, at least, that's what Shana gave as a reason. Actually, she didn't want to go home to an empty house. Even though she and Kincaid had been studiously avoiding getting within touching range, the tension still existed. She did wonder about his mood, however, how quiet he'd become. He would sit in the living room each evening watching the fire but just as enraptured with the tree. They'd had a lot of fun decorating it, with Emma "helping" with the lower limbs. They had invited Dylan to come, too, and had listened to Christmas music and drunk hot cocoa.

Shana remembered her childhood. Christmas was the one time everything seemed okay at home. Her mother loved the holiday and went all out decorating for it. Traditions. Shana wanted that for Emma. Good memories to recall when she was an adult.

Shana watched Gavin play with her daughter. That was the gift she wanted most for her daughter—

family. Siblings to grow up with and be friends with as adults.

Unconditional love—and a family that Emma could count on.

Kincaid pulled up in front of his house, his completely dark house. He pulled out his cell phone, thinking he might have missed a message from Shana, but he hadn't.

Where was she?

He pushed the garage door opener. No car inside. He went through the garage into the house, flipping on lights as he went inside. No note on the kitchen counter, which is where he would assume she would leave him a message. He checked his answering machine. Two messages, but neither was from Shana.

They were probably at Aggie's. She would've invited them to dinner if she knew he wasn't going to be home.

He busied himself. First he turned on the tree lights, then he got a fire going. He'd come home to an empty house thousands of times. It had never bothered him before. Shana and Emma had lived with him for five days and he was already used to sharing his space. Used to the noise and the company.

And used to getting up each morning and seeing a beautiful woman puttering in his kitchen, and a tiny, stubborn version of her banging her high chair tray and talking an incomprehensible blue streak....

After he got the fire started, he moved close to the tree, hypnotized by the bubble lights Shana had insisted on buying, saying they reminded her of better times. He wanted to surround the tree with gifts. He couldn't remember the last time he'd given or received a Christmas gift, except business-related. He hadn't thought it mattered, either. But now he found himself looking through catalogs and viewing websites. He'd even checked some of Emma's clothes to see what size she wore. He'd been wondering if she'd like a sled ride. They could drive to the snow and—

He spotted headlights through the trees, then Shana's car emerged. She drove straight into the garage. Relief washed over him. He'd had no reason to worry, since everyone in town knew her and someone would've notified him if there was something wrong, but some things couldn't be reasoned out. He felt responsible for her. Them.

"We're home!" Shana called out from the back of the house.

"Home!" Emma shouted, too.

It made him smile. He moved toward the kitchen doorway, meeting them there.

"You're back early," she said. "How'd it go?"

"Very well. I'll tell you in a bit. You're late."

"We stopped by to see Gavin and Becca, then they invited us for dinner."

She shrugged off her jacket, which he took so that she could take care of Emma's. He hung them both on the rack.

"They're going to keep Emma overnight on Saturday," she said.

"They are? Why?"

"They want to practice—or so they said."

"You think they have other reasons?" He followed Emma to the tree. She loved to pull ornaments off so that she could hang them again. The bottom half was filled with non-breakables. "Like what?"

"They want me to go clubbing in Sacramento or something. Have fun, or some such nonsense."

He was caught between laughing at her tone of voice and annoyance that her brother and sister-in-law were trying to force her into the singles world, which could lead to dating. "Is that what you're going to do?"

"I'm considering my options."

"Are you going to be comfortable having Emma gone overnight?"

"No." She smiled and shrugged. "Which is why I'll probably only go as far as the Stompin' Grounds. I'll want to be in easy range."

"I'll go with you, if you want."

She was quiet a few seconds. "I'm going to ask Aggie."

"All done," Emma said, handing him an ornament she'd pulled off. She toddled over to the fireplace. "Hot," she said, holding out her hands, then she shivered, imitating what Shana often did to make her daughter laugh.

"Yes, it's very hot," Shana said. "Come sit with me, peapod. Let's enjoy the fire and the tree for a little while before bedtime."

Kincaid added ambiance to the moment by turning on some Christmas music while Emma snuggled in with her mother. She'd started smiling at him now and then, but she still wouldn't let him lift her out of her high chair or into her car seat. It was beginning to bother him that she wasn't warming up to him the way she did with other people.

Like Dylan, whom she'd seemed to adore from the first moment.

Emma fell asleep almost instantly, so Shana carried her upstairs and put her to bed.

"I think I'll have some brandy," he said when Shana returned. "Want some?"

"I've never had it. Maybe a taste."

He splashed some into a small snifter and passed it to her to take the first sip. She tasted it tentatively then wrinkled her nose. "Ugh."

She gave it back to him with a lopsided smile and sat on the sofa again. She'd replaced her shoes with fuzzy pink slippers and had brushed her hair. He thought he smelled lemons and realized she had to have put on some perfume. He wanted to sniff her neck. He wanted to sit on the couch with her, put his arms around her and watch the fire together. He settled for sitting at the opposite end of the sofa instead of in his chair.

"Can I ask you a question?" she said.

"Sure."

"How long has it been since you've had a Christmas tree?"

He wasn't certain he wanted to take a trip down memory lane, but he answered her, anyway. "This would be my first."

"Ever?"

"In my whole life."

"That's really sad."

"It is." He sipped his brandy and thought about it. "We lived in trailers most of the time. No room for a tree. No money, anyway. My father drank it all away— what little there was. When my mom reached her breaking point, she took off. I never heard from her directly after that. We were notified of her death a couple of years later."

"How horrible!"

He didn't want to think about. "That's when I emancipated myself and got out, too."

"What's involved in emancipation?"

"You have to have a job, a place to live and parental permission. And you have to stay in school. Plus, I had to convince a judge I was better off on my own. I'd been to this area once in middle school on a field trip about the gold rush. I never forgot it."

"Who gave you a job?"

"Aggie's late husband, John. He offered me a room in their house, too, but they still had five kids at home, and I needed time alone, so I rented a room from June Morrison."

"The librarian?"

"She was kind and quiet. I studied hard, I worked harder and I kept my nose clean."

Shana heard so much more than just the spoken words. She heard his pain at his mother's abandonment and his father's abuses. She heard pride in his ability to take care of himself. Above all, she heard strength and confidence. He'd overcome a lot to get to this level of success.

She vowed to make this Christmas truly special for

him. He might be a man who had everything money could buy, but he couldn't buy memories.

"Don't feel sorry for me," he said into her long silence. "I don't."

Shana slid down the sofa until she was next to him. She tucked an arm under his and leaned her head against his shoulder. "What a lot of deep, dark secrets people keep hidden from the world," she said, feeling his cheek settle against her hair.

"You smell like lemons."

"You smell like brandy."

A few beats passed. "Is that bad?" he asked finally.

"No. It's just different. You usually smell like the outdoors, and sometimes like wood smoke."

He lifted his arm and settled it around her. They both went quiet for a while, then she said, "Until I came back last year I'd spent ten years roaming the world. I lived in hostels mostly, and tents a lot. Occasionally a hotel room, sometimes even a swanky one, if we'd befriended the right person along the way. The last place was a shack on a farm in Spain." She swallowed. "I don't want that life for my daughter. You've given me stability, and a chance for me to build a future for my daughter and me. I don't know how to repay you for that."

"We?" he asked, backtracking on what she'd said.

"Me and Richard. Emma's father. He died of bacterial meningitis before I knew I was pregnant. It was so quick. Healthy, then gone."

"I'm sorry."

"Me, too. Especially for Emma. He was a fun-loving, kind and totally irresponsible man."

"Yet you loved him."

"I did. But toward the end, I'd gotten restless. I wanted to root somewhere, and he still wanted to wander." She'd surprised herself by moving next to Kincaid when she'd struggled for days to keep her distance. And he was surprising her now by just holding her. "We were loners who found each other. We didn't gather a lot of friends along the way."

She still hadn't, she thought. She was stuck in that mode. It wasn't a good example for Emma.

"Do his parents know about Emma?"

"They don't believe she's his. I probably got pregnant a few days before he died. And she was overdue. So…" She snuggled closer to Kincaid, close enough to feel the beat of his heart against his chest. "I hope they want to meet her sometime, but I'm okay with it for now, especially knowing what I know of them, which isn't good. Emma's got lots of family here."

It was barely eight o'clock, but suddenly Shana was exhausted. She'd been working hard physically for three days, much harder than she usually did. And it was comfortable here in front of the fire, being held against his warm, firm body. She rested a hand on his chest to keep from sliding, then closed her eyes. He encircled her with his other arm, slid his hand up and down her arm in a soothing and yet arousing way. His heart beat a little louder, a little faster.

What are we doing here, Kincaid? The words stayed trapped in her head. She'd made the move, getting closer to him out of sympathy for his heartbreaking childhood. His had been much worse than hers, which was more a case of being ignored than abused. She could learn from him.

"How'd you do it?" she asked.

"Do what?"

His breath was warm against her hair. She realized how comfortable she'd gotten with him, dangerously so. She sat up and moved away, immediately feeling cold and a little lost.

"How did you let go of the past?" she asked. "I need to do that, and I can't seem to."

"I didn't for a long time. It was something Aggie said after her husband's funeral. I was barely legal age and the man who'd given me my break had died. I was going to have to make it on my own somehow. She said if I kept going through life with that chip on my shoulder, I was never going to be able to stand up straight and look someone in the eye so they knew I was telling the truth. 'You need to forgive your parents,' she said. She made me say it to her right then. 'I forgive you, Mom and Dad.'"

"That's all it took?"

"All? It was the hardest damn thing I'd ever done. It felt like I had a mouth full of rocks. Aggie made me repeat it until I could say it straight out and clearly. By then, I really had forgiven them. Although I never forget," he added quietly. "It's not that it doesn't haunt me sometimes, but I can deal with it."

"Why have you kept to yourself so much?"

"I figured if anyone knew where—who—I'd come

from, they would think less of me. It took time and maturity to get past that. By then, it'd become a habit being a loner."

"And now?"

"I've been trying to be more open. I've accepted invitations to go to parties and barbecues, things like that."

"Why has it become important now?"

He cocked his head. "Why all the questions?"

"I'm trying to understand you. Now that I've spent time with you, I think some of the ideas I've had in my head about you are wrong."

"Like what?"

"Like why you pursued my sister when you knew she and Joe were meant for each other." There. She'd gotten it out in the open, that hurdle she hadn't been able to get past with him.

"Dixie?" he said, looking shocked. Then he shook his head. "Dixie and I became friends, good friends, while I remodeled her shop, but that's all."

She tried to analyze his expression. He'd always seemed to be honest with her, so why would he be lying this time?

"Is that why you've always been irritated with me?" he asked intently.

She shrugged. "That's part of it, I guess. I didn't respect you for going after a woman who so clearly belonged to someone else."

"Ask Dixie, if you don't believe me. We did talk about it, because she'd thought the same thing. I hadn't had a woman friend before, not a close one. She misread me. We got it squared away. I like her. I also admire her. There's nothing more to it."

"If I talk to Dixie she'll think it's because I'm interested in you myself."

He just stared at her, asking a question without saying the words aloud.

She squirmed, hedging the truth some. "Of course you interest me, Kincaid. But I don't want to risk what we have going here."

"It's getting harder every day not to touch you," he said, reaching for her pink-slippered feet and pulling them into his lap. He waited long enough that she could've pulled her feet back, then he tossed her slippers to the floor and began massaging her feet. "Close your eyes and enjoy it," he said.

She curled her toes. "I don't want to get used to this."

"This?"

"This comfort. This ease." She paused. "This excitement. I'm doing everything for you that a wife does, except sleeping with you."

"Dammit, Shana. Just lie back and relax. If I'd wanted to seduce you into my bed, I would have done so by now."

"Well, that's a little egotistical, don't you think?"

"It's the truth." He looked annoyed. "You know, it's very hard to do something nice for you. You're always suspicious of motive."

He was right, of course. But she wasn't suspicious of anyone except him. What did that say?

"Chicken," he said with a challenging grin. He still hadn't released her feet, and she still hadn't relaxed them.

She finally shoved a pillow under her head and stretched out. "Okay, but don't blame me if you get all excited."

"Okay, but feel free to blame me if *you* do."

She peeked at him, then settled in. "As if. I get massages now and then at Dixie's spa. It's never turned me on."

"You haven't had one from me."

He sounded too sure of himself, but it was only her feet, after all, hardly an erogenous zone for her.

Or so she thought.

He manipulated her toes, pushed deeply into her arches, and rotated her ankles, all normal foot massage techniques, but there was something about *how* he was doing it. His work-calloused hands added a new dimension, rubbing her skin differently from soft, lotion-covered hands. And he had a way of teasing her skin with his fingertips even as his hands massaged deeply. And then he let his fingers drift up her legs, almost to her calves, dragging them down slowly, pressing down, lengthening her muscles, tight from going up and down a ladder much of the day.

And it felt so good, so relaxing…so arousing. She moaned a little, wriggled a little. Her foot slid over the placket of his jeans as she moved, revealing he was aroused, too.

"Not blaming you," he said quietly but with a certain amount of humor.

She opened her eyes a little. "I *am* blaming you."

He changed then. His expression darkened. His hands moved farther up her legs beneath her jeans. He tickled the backs of her knees, making her arch up. He dragged her onto his lap so that she straddled him then began to massage her back through her shirt. She could've said no anytime, could've climbed off him, but she stayed, enjoying the first sensual touch she'd experienced in two years.

He eased her forward so that her face was tucked against his neck, her chest against his, then he stroked her back with strong fingers, loosening every muscle while at the same time exciting her more than she thought imaginable. He slid his hands down her rear, cupped her there and settled her differently on him, so that she could feel his hard ridge of arousal pressing against her, even through two layers of jeans.

It was the layers separating them that finally woke her up to reality. They needed to keep those layers between them. The only way this relationship, this job, could work was if they didn't give in to their desire. There was too much at stake, too much to lose, especially for her.

She pulled back, was tempted to kiss him, but didn't. She climbed off him.

"I'm sorry," she said, meaning it in every way. She headed to the stairs, feeling wrung out.

"A pool's been started about us," he said.

She stopped, turned around.

He came up beside her. "I just thought you should know."

"Do you know the specifics?"

"Whether we'll be sleeping together by Christmas."

She crossed her arms. People were betting on exactly

what she wanted for herself, except she didn't want to wait as long as Christmas. "And how exactly would anyone know if that happened?"

"How does anyone know anything in this town? Maybe one way would be to wait a few months beyond Christmas and see if you end up pregnant, then count back."

"Haven't they heard of birth control? The very last thing that can happen is that I get pregnant. I can't bring another pregnancy upon myself and my parents. My mom and I are getting along okay. That would end that."

He said nothing. She didn't know what to make of it.

"I am sorry, Kincaid. For all that you've given me, I don't seem to be able to repay you with anything of value. I didn't mean to tease you." She gestured toward the couch, feeling as if they should clear the air.

"You're repaying me with exactly what I expected when I hired you—good, hard work. As for that," he said, pointing as she had to the sofa, "I enjoyed it, but it was good that you stopped it. I'll keep better control from now on."

Disappointment landed on Shana with a thud. In some ways, she wished he would just take charge, not be sensitive to her wish to keep her reputation spotless. And yet, she wouldn't admire him for that. What a tangled web....

"Good night, Shana."

"Night."

An hour later, she heard him come upstairs and go

to his bedroom. What had he been doing? Watching television? Staring at the tree?

Wondering how to get rid of her now that she'd become a complication?

He felt responsible for her now. She needed to hold up her end of the bargain.

Chapter Ten

On Saturday night, Shana drove into the parking lot of the Stompin' Grounds, pulled into a space, then before she'd shifted into Park, backed out and left. "This is crazy," she muttered. She didn't want to be there. She didn't want her baby girl to sleep somewhere other than in her own bed tonight, within hearing range.

"Now what?" she asked herself as she drove north, thinking she would head to Grass Valley instead, away from the watchful eyes and betting pool of Chance City.

It had been hard leaving Emma, hard enough to make Shana cry. Plus, she was going out alone because Aggie had a date with Doc. Aggie had suggested two of her granddaughters, but they both had plans.

Everyone had a date—or a husband—except her. She hadn't even thought about it before, but no one had asked her out since she'd moved to town. No one had even seemed interested. That was pretty depressing in itself. She must give off a leave-me-alone vibe she wasn't aware of. She knew she was defensive about her independence, about not wanting to rely on anyone, but that didn't mean she didn't want to have fun.

Except…that was clearly what everyone thought.

Determined to change that misconception, Shana found a turnaround and headed back to the Stompin' Grounds, where she would know people and could find someone to share a table with or a game of pool. She was pretty good with a cue stick.

If only she liked beer. She hated the stuff, but she figured the country bar and grill probably didn't offer strawberry margaritas, which would leave her with no choice but beer.

It'd been hard leaving Kincaid at home, too. She would've liked his company for her first night without Emma, but the past couple of days had been tension-filled enough. They'd been cordial to each other, acting as if nothing had happened between them, but her dreams were full of him at night, and during the day she couldn't be within a few feet of him without her body almost attaching itself to his.

It was a dangerous situation for her, although he seemed to be managing just fine.

Which really ticked her off.

Shana greeted two smokers standing by the front door to the bar, then she went inside. It was noisy, but in a good way. Music and laughter mingled. The sound of pool balls clacking punctuated the din. Even though she'd never been here, the bartender welcomed her by name, so she took a seat at the bar and ordered a hamburger and a beer.

People waved, many she knew by sight if not by name. The hamburger was good, the music made her sway and the beer wasn't as bad as she remembered. She kept eyeing the pool table, hoping for a turn. She recognized Big Dave Gunderson. He'd been a friend of Gavin's in high school, which meant he'd also graduated with Kincaid. He'd been called Big Dave since middle school, being taller and broader than any other boy. He still was.

He'd also taken Kincaid's date home last week.

He gave her the eye now and then when it wasn't his turn to shoot. When she finished her meal, he wandered over. Or moseyed over, she thought, a definite cowboy sort of swagger in his step. His hair was a little shaggy, his jaw soft and his teeth unusually white, as if he'd just had them bleached.

"Howdy, Shana," he said, touching his forehead as if tipping a hat.

"Hey, Dave. How're you?"

"I was feelin' a little down until you walked in. Sure picked up my spirits seeing you, especially since I don't recall you coming here before."

"It's my first time."

"A virgin, huh?"

Shana hid her wince by taking a swig of her beer rather than answer. "Maybe I could get in on a game?"

"You play?"

"Not in years, but I used to be competent."

"I'm sure the guys'll take a seat long enough for you to have a shot at it. C'mon, darlin'."

He waited for her to go ahead of him, and she could feel his eyes following her every move. She'd bet he'd stand behind her while she played, too, getting a good look at her butt, trying to throw her off her game if he could.

He racked the balls and offered her the opening shot with a courtly bow.

Shana ran the table.

Kincaid pulled into the parking lot of the Stompin' Grounds at midnight. He'd been in bed but not asleep when Tom, the bartender/owner, had called saying he thought Kincaid should come drive Shana home before she did something she might regret in the morning.

"Like what?" Kincaid had asked.

"She's only bought two beers the whole night, but the way she's acting I think maybe she's been sippin' off of Big Dave's, too. She's just being…rowdy."

Kincaid only needed to hear the words "Big Dave." He was dressed and out of the house in less than a minute. Before he hopped in his truck, he peeled off the magnetic ad signs from his doors, transforming his vehicle into one like many others in the bar's parking lot. He backed in right next to Shana's SUV.

He didn't have to wait long before the door opened and Shana came out—with Big Dave. And she was looking up at the man and laughing.

Kincaid gripped the door handle.

They trudged through the dirt-and-crushed-rock

parking lot. Big Dave put his hands on her shoulders and steered her toward her car.

Kincaid had never seen her laugh so much. It annoyed the hell out of him.

And he sure wasn't going to let her car end up in front of Big Dave's house overnight for all the town to see.

He climbed out of his truck as they reached Shana's car.

"Kincaid," she said, surprise quickly transforming into a big grin. "Pool table is free, if you're interested."

"She left a lot of shattered egos in there," Dave said. "She only lost one game all night."

"Yeah, well, I was out of practice."

Dave guffawed at that.

"What are you doing here?" she asked Kincaid.

"I heard through the grapevine that you needed a ride home."

"Me? Why? I've only had two glasses of beer over four hours. I didn't even finish the last one. I'm fine. Who called to tell you that?"

"It doesn't matter."

She raised her brows but said nothing, probably because Dave was way too curious.

"I told her I'd see her safely home," Dave said, his chest puffed up as if daring Kincaid to comment about last weekend's date debacle.

"Well, I'm here now. I'll take over. She *is* going to my house, after all."

"You okay with lord and master here taking over, darlin'?" Dave asked Shana.

She giggled a little. "Yes. Thanks, Dave. You've been a real gentleman."

"I aim to please." He gave her a little salute, but his expression turned smug when he added a good-night to Kincaid. He sauntered off, got in his truck and drove away.

"Thanks so much for ruining the first fun I've had in a long time," Shana said, crossing her arms, her eyes spitting fire.

"I got a call. I answered it."

"Who called?"

"Someone who was concerned about you." He held up a hand as she started to protest. "I won't tell you, so just give it up. Let's go."

"Did you think I was going home with him?" she asked.

He walked away, got in his truck, started his engine and waited, grateful that she wasn't the least bit drunk. When she finally did start her car, he relaxed. Then she took twenty minutes to make the ten-minute drive to his house, meandering through various neighborhoods as if out for a Sunday drive.

He didn't find it funny at all. The image of her spending the night with Big Dave ruined his mood.

Would it matter if it was someone other than Dave? came a loud question in his head.

"I'm responsible for her," he muttered as he followed her up his driveway. By the time she'd parked in the garage, he was already in the house. She came through the kitchen door, gave him a cool look then marched toward the stairs.

"My date last weekend went home with him, then spent the night," he said.

"I heard." She kept climbing the stairs. "I'm not her."

"You looked cozy with him." She'd never laughed with *him* like that.

"I was having fun! You stole that from me." She reached the top of the staircase.

He was a couple of steps behind her, caught up to her as she went in her bedroom and hurled her purse on the bed, saying, "Get out."

"He was touching you." He'd lost all perspective but couldn't seem to stop himself.

"You've touched me more." She threw up her hands. "I have no interest in sleeping with him. Not that it's any of your business."

He moved closer, grateful for her admission, but still not sure he believed her. "I've seen for myself just how hot you are."

"Only for you!" she shouted.

Her words had the effect of dynamite blasting inside him.

She made a sound of frustration, a kind of low growl. She undoubtedly hadn't intended to tell him that, just as he hadn't intended to show how jealous he was. But the words were out there now, unchecked.

What next?

They stood like duelists, eyeing each other, waiting for someone to make the first move.

"I really want to sleep with you," she said as if she were drowning and it was her last breath.

He didn't want to give her time to think about it, to

see how their relationship would change forever. How, in fact, their relationship could end. But all those logical thoughts swirled in his brain like a tornado, tossing and turning, not connecting to the sensible core of him.

He reached for her, pulled her close and kissed her. She came back at him without hesitation, demanding, encouraging and arousing. He didn't have to stop this time, didn't even have to slow down. He only had to satisfy and be satisfied....

Shana lunged at him, ran her hands over him, struggled to breathe. He tasted like every fantasy she'd had about him, hot and exciting. She dove her fingers into his hair and gripped his head as he unfastened her shirt, then her jeans. Hands were in motion, bodies moving to accommodate, then they were both naked, standing beside her bed.

"You're perfect," he said, low and hushed.

She'd only been with Richard, and he hadn't looked anything like Kincaid, whose years of physical labor had given him a sculpted, muscular body. He had broad shoulders, a chest lightly dusted with hair, narrow hips, long, sturdy legs—and the fascinatingly all-male part of him that flattered her with expectation and invitation.

He didn't give her time to explore but pulled her down onto the bed and joined with her, filling her, stretching her. Then he went perfectly still, holding his weight off her, his eyes closed, his body shaking. He lowered himself slowly, ducked his head to take her nipple into his mouth. She arched and cupped his head, feeling vibration under her hands from the needy sounds he made.

And then she stopped noticing anything but the building pressure, the escalating pleasure. He finally began to move. She wrapped her legs around him, matching his rhythm. He sought her mouth with his just as she peaked, the explosion powerful, like nothing she'd experienced. Then just as she was coming down, he surged, escalated—

"Wait! Stop!" She tried to push him away. "Kincaid! I'm not on the pill."

He pulled out, but he was too far gone. He landed on her, his body taut and still moving, groans of completion coming from him.

After a few seconds he rolled onto his side. She put a hand over her mouth. "I'm so sorry. I wasn't thinking...."

"Neither was I." He was breathing hard, looking a little bewildered. "I assumed, since you'd mentioned birth control before. I should've asked."

"No, it's my fault completely. Are you okay?"

"Okay, how?"

"You know. Being interrupted like that." She didn't know how to ask him about it.

"You're blushing," he said, tracing her cheeks with his fingers, his expression serious. "I have to be honest. There's a chance I didn't pull out in time. I can't tell for sure."

"I can't be pregnant. I just can't." How could she prove she'd grown up if she got pregnant out of wedlock again? And this time it would be to a man who didn't love her. Richard had loved her, would've married her in a flash.

Or would he? She needed to think about that. He'd never brought up marriage except in negative ways. Would having Emma have made a difference?

Kincaid rubbed her arm. "It won't be an issue, Shana. We'll get married."

He said it so matter-of-factly, as if it was something simple, when it was anything but. She stalled by pulling up an afghan from the foot of the bed and draping it over them.

"We won't know for a couple of weeks. People will count," she said. Everyone would know.

"Then we'll get married tomorrow."

"T-tomorrow? But—"

"But what? Even if people guess, they'll never know for sure." He was propped up on an elbow, watching her.

"You're talking about marriage as if we're going to movies and just need to figure which one to see. It's not that easy. People get married for…" She stopped because the first word that came to mind was *love*. People get married for love.

"Lots of reasons," he said, finishing her sentence.

"We fight."

"We disagree in a lively way."

"I have a daughter already."

"Who needs a father, don't you think? Why not me?"

Emma hadn't fully accepted him, however, which complicated the issue.

"In my mind, Shana, pregnancy is an excellent reason to marry, for everyone involved."

"I need to think about this."

"You can think all you want. It's not going to change the outcome. My parents never married. That won't happen to any child of mine." He got out of bed and headed for the door. "I'll be back in ten minutes. Do your thinking."

She got out of bed as soon as he disappeared, shutting herself in the bathroom. She washed her face, brushed her teeth, dragged a warm washcloth down her body. She tried to think, but every thought dead ended. Finally she put on her robe and returned to her bedroom. He was sitting on the side of her bed, naked. Waiting for a decision.

He shook his head at her, slowly, surely, as he got to his feet and came to her.

"No robes. No nightgowns. Nothing." He untied her robe and slipped it off her shoulders, then tossed it aside. He took her hand in his and lead her down the hall.

It seemed absurd to be walking naked, hand in hand, and yet she clung to him. They reached his bedroom but kept walking into the bathroom. He'd filled his spa tub, the one with the jets she'd been dying to try, particularly now that she was working so hard physically every day.

He held her hand as she stepped into the tub, then got in behind her. She nestled against him, feeling not just comfortable, but safe. He hit the button to start the jets, and the bubbles instantly began to soothe her fragile nerves. His arms encircled her, his hands coming to rest on her belly. She closed her eyes at the reminder of what the future could hold.

"I can't get married without Dixie," she said.

His chest hardened, the only clue to the fact he'd had a reaction to what she'd said.

"Has she said when she'll be home?"

"She hopes by Christmas."

"That's two weeks."

"I know."

"We can't wait two weeks, not if you want the town to believe you weren't pregnant when we got married."

"I may not be. In fact, I'm probably not. Really, what are the odds?" She was still having a hard time grasping the fact he would so easily marry her, even without knowing whether she was pregnant. What did that mean? Had he fallen for her? She knew he was as attracted physically as she was, but was there more? And if so, why wasn't he telling her how he felt?

And how do you feel about him? came an insistent question in her head. She'd come to respect him a great deal, appreciate him and maybe, just maybe, she'd fallen in love with him.

She'd been thinking about him all night at the bar. How much she wished he'd been there, how she enjoyed his company…how she couldn't wait to see him every morning and sit with him every evening by the fire. She hadn't wanted to give in to those feelings—unless he felt the same. And she worried a little that she appreciated so much what he'd done for her, she'd turned it into love in her head.

But now, lying here in his arms, naked, she knew it wasn't just appreciation.

"When can you take one of those home pregnancy tests?" he asked after their long silence.

"I'm not sure. Probably two weeks, *if* I haven't started my period by then, anyway, which would make this all a moot point."

"Except that you could be two weeks pregnant by then. And unmarried."

He really is pushing marriage, not just suggesting or offering it. He wants to get married. Why?

At the very least, they needed a cooling-off period, she decided. Everything was happening way too fast for comfort. And she wanted to marry for love.

"How about this?" she said. "On Christmas Eve, two weeks from today, I'll do a home test—if it seems necessary at that point. Dixie should be home around then, and if you and I decide marriage is the right thing to do, we'll get married right away, but with our family and friends in attendance. We won't elope with just Dixie and Joe as witnesses, okay?"

"Whatever you want."

I want to hear what you really think, what you want to do, not what you think you should *do.*

He slid his hands up her body, cupped her breasts. She sucked in a breath as he thumbed her nipples.

"Stay with me tonight," he said close to her ear.

She didn't have to think about it more than a millisecond. "Yes. As long as you have—"

"Protection. I do."

Shana was struck by a tsunami of jealousy. He'd

slept with other women. Really, it was ridiculous to think he hadn't, and yet she couldn't stand the idea of it. In her mind, the only way of fixing that was to make love with him like no one else ever had, wiping out every memory of every woman he'd ever been with.

Just remember he never married any of them, she reminded herself. *You're special to start with.*

Not special, she thought, but careless, and he was too much of a gentleman not to make an honest woman of her. It was the most incredible thing anyone had ever done for her.

She turned to face him, straddling him, needing to kiss him. Everything had happened so fast earlier. She want to go slowly, to cherish.

She discovered him fully aroused when she settled herself against him. She loved the feel of him pressed against her, loved how his lips captured hers and his tongue explored her mouth, and how he held her face. When he made a trail with his lips down to her breasts she tipped her head back, giving him better access. He knew just the right combination of things to do with his mouth to have her climbing, gasping, struggling to hold back so that he could join her.

Instead, he rocked against her, sucked her nipple in his mouth, squeezed her other breast and sent her over the edge, her moans echoing in the tile room. When she finally opened her eyes, he looked fierce, intense. Hungry.

"Let's go to bed," she said.

He toweled her dry, taking his time, even though he

was aroused the whole time. "Did you nurse Emma?" he asked, brushing the towel over her breasts.

"I tried, but wasn't successful. The nurse at the women's shelter where I was living told me I was probably too stressed."

He stopped using the towel on her then. "You were living at a shelter? Where did you have Emma?"

"In a hospital ER. I was able to stay at the shelter for a few months after, then when someone donated a car, the shelter's board members gave it to me so that I could come home."

He kissed her softly, tenderly. "You're a survivor."

"So are you. Most people are when they have no choice. And I had the extra incentive of Emma." She took him by the hand. "Come on. We only have this night alone. Let's make the most of it."

They stopped beside the bed. He'd already turned down the linens. A condom packet was on the nightstand. "Only one?" she asked pertly.

He pulled open the drawer, showing her they weren't limited to one.

"Well, let's get this show started." She shoved him onto the bed, then followed him down. "Ladies first."

His smile came, slow and sexy. "Be my guest."

And she was. For the whole rest of the night.

Chapter Eleven

Kincaid woke up in the morning disappointed that Shana wasn't next to him—and also relieved. In the harsh light of day, their situation was bound to look different. He needed a few minutes to consider everything that had happened.

He stroked the sheet where she'd slept, then tucked his hands behind his head and stared at the ceiling. In one sense he wasn't surprised they'd ended up in bed together. That was a situation waiting, if not begging, to happen. Put a couple who desire each other within proximity and the inevitable will eventually occur. That it had happened so soon was a surprise. That they'd put themselves in a position of possibly having to get married was a shock.

He wasn't a careless man, and she'd had plenty of

reasons not to forget about birth control until the last possible second—or rather a second past that point.

In one sense he'd felt numb the whole night, the unreality of potential fatherhood hovering over him, but overruled at every step by fulfilled desires.

Shana Callahan was sexy, enthusiastic and generous. When they'd finally slept, they'd wrapped themselves together, as if it was the last time.

Was it?

There'd been no talk of her sleeping with him from now on, only of taking the one night for themselves.

He cared about her more than anyone he'd met. He wanted to provide for her, to ease her burdens, to enjoy making love with her as often as possible. He liked her. He admired her, even when she'd been stubbornly independent.

Did he love her? He'd long worried he wasn't capable of love. He hadn't had positive examples in his childhood to show him how to express or feel love, and since he hadn't fallen for anyone in all the years since, he'd feared he couldn't ever love.

He wanted to, but maybe it would have to be enough that he felt other strong feelings for Shana.

"Good morning." Shana came in carrying a tray. She was dressed in her robe, her hair tucked behind her ears. "I'm glad you slept in."

He hadn't even looked at the time, which said a lot. He was usually up before daybreak. "Good morning. What have you got?"

"Sustenance. We had an active night." She smiled. "We need fuel."

She'd fixed an omelet, country fries and ham.

"It looks great, but there's way too much."

"I figured we'd share a plate. Is that okay?" She set the footed tray next to him and knelt on the opposite side. "I mean, we've shared whatever germs we might have all night, so what difference does it make?"

He laid a hand at her neck and gently pulled her forward to kiss. Her robe gapped a little, revealing the tempting inner curves of her breasts. As they kissed, he slid his hand down her chest to capture one breast then the other, loving the feel of her nipples pressing into his palms.

This was the way he wanted to wake up every day, especially when she responded so quickly, giving him a look that said dessert would follow breakfast.

They barely spoke while they ate, mostly just comments on the food, then he picked up the tray and set it on the floor next to the bed. By the time he turned around, she'd let the robe fall down her arms. She looked sweet and sexy at the same time.

He reached for her, then a phone rang.

"Hold that thought," she said, digging into her pocket for her cell phone and answering it, listening intently but climbing off the bed at the same time. "Give me ten minutes." She ended the call and headed out the door. "Emma is apparently inconsolable this morning. I need to go to her."

"I'll come, too."

She stopped in the hallway. "I'm not sure that's the best idea. You can be sure Big Dave has talked about your encounter last night. If we show up this morning together…"

"If we wait until the last minute to start showing up together around town, people aren't going to believe we got married because we wanted to, not because you were pregnant."

She winced at that. He reran his words in his head, trying to understand why that bothered her.

"Okay," she said, but wearily. "We'll have to take my car. I don't want to take the time to transfer her car seat to your truck."

They were out of the house in five minutes, reached Gavin and Becca's house five minutes later. They could hear Emma crying as they rushed up the path to the front door, which Gavin opened before they reached it. They went straight inside.

"Mama!" Emma cried out, opening her arms, trying to fling herself from Becca to Shana.

"I'm here, baby. It's okay."

Kincaid watched, fascinated, as Emma wrapped her arms and legs around Shana and burrowed herself against her mother. She heaved a few shuddering breaths, her whole body quivering as she tried to calm down. After a minute she opened her eyes and spotted him.

What now? Would she start crying all over again? Turn away from him? Ignore him?

"Kinky," she said with a watery smile. "My Kinky."

That was it. She had him lock, stock and barrel. She owned his heart forevermore. It was scary as hell. "Hello, Miss Emma. Are you doing okay now?"

She nodded.

"I'll bet you had fun with Uncle Gavin and Aunt Becca."

She nodded again, then looked their way as they stood arm-in-arm, brave smiles on their faces.

"Ready for parenthood?" he asked them, laughing a little.

"We'll get out of your hair so that you can relax," Shana said. She hugged each of them. Emma gave sloppy kisses. "Thank you for keeping her. Really. I didn't think I was going to be able to handle it, but it was okay. I knew she was in good hands."

As Shana and Becca headed outside, Gavin's hand came down on Kincaid's shoulder. "I heard you had a little run-in with Big Dave last night."

"*Already* you heard that?"

Gavin shrugged, as if to say, "You know this town."

"We didn't come to fists or anything." He watched Shana laugh with Becca as she buckled Emma in. Shana had her girl back. She'd relaxed.

"Did you have a good night, too?" Gavin asked. When he didn't answer, Gavin said, "My sister has a glow about her this morning. Or maybe it's just her messy hair—and yours—that gives it away."

Kincaid met his glance but remained silent. He'd meant what he said to Shana—they couldn't just spring it on people that they got married, if it came to that. They needed to set the scene ahead of time.

"Doesn't surprise me," Gavin added quietly as they walked out to the car. "I saw it months ago when you and she worked on Becca's condo."

And Dylan had noticed the attraction, too. So, maybe no one would be surprised, which was probably why there was a pool under way.

"I approve, if that matters to you," Gavin added before they got within hearing range of the women.

Kincaid still didn't say anything. Until he knew for sure what was going to happen, he didn't want anyone thinking it was a done deal between him and Shana. But he did shake Gavin's hand before he got into the SUV and headed home.

Home. Suddenly it had a whole new meaning to him.

On Monday morning, Shana carried Emma up Aggie's walkway before she headed to Nevada City to meet with a new client. Excitement lightened her step. Kincaid had met with a man last week who wanted a master bedroom remodel, and he was willing to let Shana come aboard with design ideas.

The anticipation took her mind off Kincaid and all that had happened in the past couple of days, if that was possible. She'd slept in his bed again last night. It had felt…right.

"Good morning, Shana," Doc Saxon said at the door, his eyes twinkling. "Aggie's in the kitchen."

"Did you have a sleepover, Doc?" Shana asked with a wink. "I didn't see your car out front."

He pretended to twist a key into his lips. "Hello, Emma. How are you today?"

"Aggie," Emma said, her tone indicating she was not happy about the change in her routine. Aggie always met her at the door.

"She's in the kitchen, sweetheart."

Shana put Emma down and she raced off.

"Your friend Kincaid sure seems to be gaining some notoriety these days," Doc said. "The Stompin' Grounds must be a bad influence on him."

Before she could respond, Aggie and Emma came into the room. Emma was clutching a ball almost as big as her head.

"Look," she said, although it sounded like "wook."

"Jim picked it up for her," Aggie said.

"You're bribing children to like you now?" Shana asked Doc.

"Maybe."

Shana raised her brows. "Does that mean you'll be here a lot when Emma's here?"

"Maybe."

"We have a question for you," Aggie said. "Is it possible to take two houses full of furniture and mingle them into one so that it feels right to both people?"

"Is that your way of telling me you're getting married?" Shana bubbled inside at the possibility. Aggie had been alone for such a long time.

"Well, we can't very well live together, can we? What kind of message would we be sending our children and grandchildren?" Aggie said.

Shana jumped up and down. She pulled Aggie into a big hug, then included Doc. Emma raised her hands, wanting up to join them.

"This is the best news ever," Shana said. "I'm so happy for you both. And yes, it's possible to do what you asked. I'd be happy to take on the task, if you'll let me. I'd love to pay you back somehow for everything you've done for me."

"We'd be honored," Doc said. "Now. There's more. We're not telling the family until Christmas Eve at the town party. You'll keep it secret until then, right?"

"Of course. Emma, too, right, peapod?"

Emma nodded seriously.

"I guess I can't start until you've made your announcement, but I can come up with a plan. Maybe I could come see your house this afternoon, Doc. I know you downsized when you retired and Gavin got your old house, but I would need to do an inventory and take some pictures. I'd do the same here at Aggie's."

"I'm renting a two-bedroom place, and it's overflowing," Doc said. "Maybe we're being optimistic when we say we can mix our furniture. Maybe we need new, instead. We're counting on you for an honest opinion."

"When will you get married?"

Doc took Aggie's hand, his smile loving. "We won't be wasting any time. You get this house fixed up—it's the only one big enough to hold our families for holidays—and we'll have a simple ceremony and be done with it."

"Simple meaning a couple hundred people," Aggie said, patting his cheek.

"We'll see," he said.

Shana knew who would win that particular battle. In fact, she bet the whole town would end up being invited. Doc had been Chance City's only doctor for forty years. Aggie was well known and beloved.

Shana made her farewells and drove to Nevada City

to meet the new client, a man in his fifties who needed better access for his wheelchair, as his health was rapidly declining. Kincaid had built an entry ramp into his house a couple years ago.

The client liked her ideas, so she was on a high when she got back to town. She stopped in where Kincaid and Dylan were putting the finishing touches on Joe and Dixie's remodel. They would be done by mid-afternoon, then Shana would set the furnishings in place. Having had the luxury of six months to do the job whenever he had time, Kincaid had updated the kitchen, added a second story, enlarged the rear of the house to include a big family room and built on a covered deck. Joe's landscaping crew had kept up the yard.

"Hello!" she called out from the living room.

"In the kitchen," Dylan shouted.

She found them installing wrought-iron cabinet door handles.

"Dixie is going to be so happy with this," Shana said. The room was contemporary yet with a rustic feel, right down to the farmhouse sink. "You do beautiful work," she said to Kincaid, who smiled at her in an entirely different way than he used to.

She tried hard not to look like a besotted fool in front of Dylan. "Mr. Broadburn says we're hired." She could hardly contain herself. "He also says he'll pay a bonus if we can escalate the process."

"I'd already planned to. He needs to be able to shower easily. I can only imagine how hard it is for him now." He wandered over, took her arm and moved her out of the kitchen, where Dylan was noisily drilling holes for the door pulls.

"How's your day been?" Kincaid asked.

She wished she could share the news about Aggie and Doc, but she'd promised not to. "It's been wonderful." She lowered her voice. "It helped that it started off so well."

He'd awakened her with soft touches and butterfly kisses. She'd kept her eyes closed and simply enjoyed until she couldn't stand it anymore and rolled over to get her fill of him. He'd been very accommodating. Then they'd laughed as he tried to change Emma's diaper, Emma frowning as he fumbled through it but otherwise cooperating.

The morning had been peaceful and tense at the same time.

He gave her a kiss now, short and sweet. "Where are you headed?"

"I have a few errands to run. Do you need me for something?"

He gave her a look that made her blush. "But if that's not possible," he said, "then maybe you could go online and research showers with wheelchair access. I'll custom build a vanity. I've only done one other handicap-accessible bathroom, and that was years ago. I'm sure there's better equipment today."

"Roger, boss."

He cocked a brow. "Right. The day you defer to me will be—"

"Boss!" Dylan shouted. "Can you take a look at this before I drill a hole in the wrong place?"

"Be right there." He tugged on Shana's hair. "I'll see you at home."

Home. His house had become that for her so quickly. If she was pregnant, it would be her home forever. If not...

Well, she wasn't going to think about that yet.

She drove to Doc's and went through each room, then checked out his garage, also stuffed with furniture. His patients had given him lots of original art through the years as payment, some of it good, some not so good, but he hadn't wanted to hurt anyone's feelings so he hadn't thrown out anything. He had enough furniture to fit into Aggie's much larger place and maybe another apartment to boot.

It would be a daunting task to move and remove furniture, one she would need help with. The entire McCoy clan would need to get involved, and that was a lot of people. Doc's children would probably come from Sacramento to help, as well.

Shana loved the spirit of Chance City, the helpfulness and even the pettiness that happened now and then.

And now that she'd come back, she never wanted to leave again.

For better or for worse, she'd found home.

Kincaid left Dylan to vacuum the kitchen floor and went to pick up a takeout order at the Lode for lunch. On his way, he spotted Shana's car in front of Doc's. Doc was one of her "errands"?

Kincaid pondered that as he picked up lunch then

headed back to Joe and Dixie's house. Shana's car was still at Doc's. The retired man could often be found sitting on his front porch, but the mid-December, rain-threatening weather would keep him inside today, probably. What were they doing? Talking about? Had she gone to him because she wasn't comfortable using her brother as her doctor?

How long had she been there? To Kincaid, an errand meant you came and went, not lingered. Was she talking to him about possibly being pregnant—and what options she had?

They hadn't talked over the weekend about not having the baby. Not once. That didn't seem like an option to her. He knew it wasn't one for him.

"Making too much of it," Kincaid told himself. After all, how did he know when she got there? Fifteen minutes ago? Twenty?

He and Dylan ate their lunch at Joe and Dixie's then headed to their next job, a sink change-out at Aggie's. Doc's house was not on his way, but he drove past it anyway. Shana's car was still there. He lived in one of Kincaid's rentals, so she wouldn't be there for a design job—and she would've told him about that. Maybe something had just come up. She would undoubtedly tell him tonight.

Kincaid had timed his trip to Aggie's for when Emma wouldn't be napping, so that the noise wouldn't wake her. He carried his toolbox, and Dylan followed with the new sink and faucets.

Aggie was holding Emma when she opened the door.

Emma looked from Kincaid to Dylan as if wondering who to greet first, then just smiled shyly.

"She just woke up," Aggie said. "If you have time, I've got apple pie fresh out of the oven. Maybe you'd like a piece before you start working."

Dylan nodded, but then looked at Kincaid for agreement.

"How about after we're done, Aggie," he said. "We just finished lunch."

Dylan tickled Emma as he walked by, leaving her giggling. They made the easy switch of old sink to new, then headed to the kitchen. Emma was chasing a ball around the room, kicking it by accident when she got close, then running to catch up with it.

"Kinky down," she said with authority. "Ball."

"Looks like I've been replaced as favorite male," Dylan said, settling at the kitchen table with a huge piece of pie and a mound of vanilla ice cream.

Kincaid sat on the floor, his legs spread open, getting Emma to do the same. They rolled the ball back and forth until Aggie offered her ice cream. Emma sat in his lap as Aggie fed her and Kincaid ate his pie. It was the first time she'd let him hold her. She wriggled a lot and clapped her hands after each bite.

Aggie smiled at him. "I'm thinking we could use a Santa for our Christmas Eve bash."

"You seem to have some sway with Doc these days," Kincaid countered, smiling back. *Do you know why Shana went to see him?*

"He's too slim."

"And I'm not?" He patted his stomach. "No bowlful of jelly here. How about Bruno? He wouldn't need padding."

Aggie laugh. "I'll tell him you said so."

Kincaid's only local competition, Bruno and he got along okay. There was enough business to go around.

"What do I owe you?" Aggie asked after they finished eating. Dylan had just taken the tools out to the truck.

"I've told you fifty times, Aggie. You'll never get a bill from me, not as long as we both shall live. It's a vow I take seriously. I wouldn't be here today if John hadn't taken me under his wing. I'm who I am because of you and John."

She kissed his cheek. "I'll keep trying."

"I'll keep turning it down."

"So, are you looking for any advice these days?"

He wondered what she knew. Had Shana talked to her? "Everything is going well, thanks." He decided to leave it at that. "Goodbye, Miss Emma."

"Bye-bye, Kinky. Bye-bye."

Kincaid ruffled her hair. Aggie helped Emma blow kisses.

A few hours later he opened his front door, stepping into a warm house, with the fireplace already going, the tree lights on and the scent of tomato and basil in the air. There were brightly wrapped presents under the tree.

"Hi," Shana said, looking pink-cheeked and happy to see him. She looked behind her, hurried over and hugged him. "I'm glad you're home."

He held her close, watching for Emma to appear,

because apparently Shana didn't want Emma observing them hugging or kissing. He wondered why. Emma wouldn't put two and two together like an adult would. Because he couldn't relax into the hug, he let her go, then saw disappointment in her eyes. *You can't have it both ways,* he wanted to say, trying to understand her thought process. He knew she was enjoying their physical relationship, but he wanted more than that. He wanted the honesty they'd promised each other when she moved in.

"Something smells good," he said instead, deciding to give her the chance to tell him about Doc on her own.

"Spaghetti and meatballs." She looked proud of herself. He'd told her only yesterday that it was his favorite meal. "I called Aggie for the recipe."

"Did you get all your errands done?" *Tell me why you were at Doc's house for so long.*

"I did. I even had time to wrap some presents."

"I noticed." He had been ordering gifts online and had them delivered to his downtown office, a safe hideaway because he hadn't given Shana the key yet, pretending he needed to get a copy made. "What else did you do?"

"Just stuff. Shopping, mostly. I picked Emma up early. We've been playing."

"I saw your car at Doc's."

She hesitated. "Oh, that. He just wanted my opinion on where to hang some art. I wasn't there long."

Yes, you were. What was she hiding?

"Kinky!" Emma came running at him. He scooped her up, stopping just short of saying, "There's my girl."

"Come. Play."

"I need to clean up first, okay?" He hadn't worked hard enough to sweat today, but he needed to escape, try to figure why Shana was keeping a secret.

"'Kay."

Still…he didn't ask Shana to go back to her own bedroom that night. He also didn't sleep as easily as he had been. What was she keeping from him? If she'd needed to talk to Doc about a possible pregnancy, why wouldn't she tell Kincaid that?

He didn't like the possible answers to that question. Not at all.

Chapter Twelve

Kincaid's business slowed down as Christmas neared, therefore so did Shana's. She wasn't disappointed about it, since it gave her time to decorate and shop. She'd finished entering all his business receipts in the computer.

She had also put in a lot of work on the Christmas Eve event tomorrow, had spent hours in the kitchen, as she was now, baking and decorating cookies to give as gifts and to put out at the party. A huge group of people would spend the whole day tomorrow decorating and cooking. The event had turned into a lot bigger production than Gavin and Becca had imagined.

Shana and Kincaid hadn't discussed the possibility she was pregnant for almost two weeks. She'd been happy, all things considered, even as she recognized she was in full avoidance mode.

She didn't want anything to change. She liked her new life.

Shana wasn't sure Kincaid felt the same. He'd become a little more distant each day—except in the bedroom. Or rather, except during sex. He didn't want to lie in bed and talk as they'd done the first couple of nights after they'd made love, but went to sleep right away, although still holding her close.

But really, what was there to say about their situation? Either she was pregnant or she wasn't, and only time would answer that question.

In the meantime, she'd fallen all the way in love with him. So had Emma, who had taken to climbing up into his lap after dinner every night. They felt like a family. Even if Shana wasn't pregnant, she wanted to marry him—although she hoped she wasn't pregnant. She still didn't want to start off that way, nor have the town know they'd been sleeping together, but the idea didn't concern her as much as it used to, either.

At the beginning she hadn't imagined major problems with living in the same house with him, not seeing beyond the antagonistic relationship they'd had. But then they'd each revealed secrets from their past, opening up. She'd gotten to know him well. She didn't see any reason that would keep them apart—unless he couldn't love her.

The front door opened and shut. She peered around the kitchen doorway, saw Kincaid and went to greet him. He'd taken off his boots on the porch.

"How'd it go?" she asked, anticipating a kiss hello.

"Fine." He went directly to the fireplace and started

building a fire. "Tables and chairs are all set up, ready to be decorated. Eric and Marcy have come up. They're staying with your brother until after Christmas."

"I know. We're invited to dinner tonight. Emma's already there, being spoiled." She moved closer. He seemed…angry. "Are you okay?"

"I don't want to go to Gavin's. You go ahead, though."

"It was your idea that we be seen together so that—"

"I know. At this point I don't think it matters." He lit the tinder, added small branches. In a few minutes he would put a couple of logs on. "We'll know tomorrow."

He might as well have plunged a knife into her heart. It was a black-and-white situation to him. He hadn't been falling in love like she had.

"Why are you so mad?" she asked him.

He hesitated a few seconds. "I'm not. I'm tired."

"You've become increasingly irritated for two weeks."

"And you've become increasingly calm."

It sounded like an accusation. "That's a bad thing?" When he didn't answer, she said, "Would you prefer I go back to my own bed?" She could hardly form the words, but she didn't know what else to do. If he wasn't going to tell her what was wrong, she had to ask questions…and get answers.

"No," he said, his voice harsh.

"Do you…want me to leave?" She swallowed around the hot lump in her throat.

He finally looked directly at her. His jaw was like iron, his eyes flinty. "No."

"Then what do you want?"

"You." One fierce word that said enough for now.

"So what's the problem?" She framed his face with her hands. "Take me. I'm yours."

He swept her into his arms and climbed the stairs, then carried her all the way down the hall to his bedroom in the most exciting, romantic gesture of her life. Then he undressed her, harsh emotions still on his face, but his hands working gently at her buttons and zipper. It felt more like a first time than their first time had, his gentleness arousing her to new heights.

It was different for her, she realized, because this time she knew she was in love.

He didn't undress but moved her onto the bed and stretched out beside her, sliding his hands over her skin, adding his lips, then his tongue. He'd come to know what excited her the most and took advantage of that now.

"I want to feel your skin next to mine," she said, grabbing his shirt. She loved the feel of his body, his warm flesh covering well-toned muscles.

"In a minute."

He continued to move down her body, touching and tasting, finally settling, bringing her pleasure, then bliss, then ecstasy, and finally such a deep satisfaction she felt like crying.

If she couldn't have him for life, she didn't know what she would do.

She gathered him close, pulling him down on her,

holding him tight. "Inside me," she whispered into his ear.

Kincaid didn't need to be asked twice. He stood to undress, not letting her help, knowing it might take him over the top way too soon. And he wanted this to last. He had a strong sense that this would be their last time, that everything would change tomorrow when she took the pregnancy test.

When he was naked, he opened the nightstand drawer.

"You don't need one," she said. "The timing is all wrong. But it's your choice, of course."

He grabbed a condom, anyway, then shut the drawer with a little more force than was necessary. He covered her body with his, not giving her a chance to touch him, or give him the same special treatment he'd just given her. He needed to be inside her. Now.

Ah, but he loved the sound she made when he joined with her, something between pleasure and relief. He kept himself still, wallowing in the feel of her, shoving all dark thoughts out of his mind, thoughts that had dogged him for weeks.

No. It was just this moment, the here and now, that mattered. Just this....

It was over way too soon. He collapsed on her, rolling onto his side after a few seconds, taking her with him. How had it come to this? How had he lived his entire adult life walking the straight and narrow, and after one night of indiscretion, be living in such turmoil?

"How can I help you?" Shana asked quietly, her face

against his chest. "Is it just the question of whether I'm pregnant or is it something else?" She angled away from him far enough to make eye contact. "Please tell me."

Isn't it all tied together? he wondered. "I feel like I've been living in limbo."

"Me, too."

"Yet you've seemed fine."

"I've focused on other things. I've loved Christmas this year. It's the first time I've had the financial freedom and enough time to make it special. I'm content here in your house. Emma's safe and happy." She ran her fingertips across his lips. "Sharing your bed has been amazing. But I can see you're not happy."

"It's just the waiting."

"I already bought the test kit. I could take it now."

He'd had the Christmas Eve deadline in his head for so long that it took a moment to think the change through. What difference would twelve hours make? If anything, they should wait until after Christmas so that they could celebrate the holiday, at least. Except…

"Okay," he said.

She left his bed and the room, returning with a small box. She went into his bathroom then didn't come out for a few minutes. When she did, she carried the test stick. She laid it on the nightstand.

"Two minutes," she said, then climbed in bed with him, burrowed close, then didn't move.

He could feel her heart pounding, felt his own match hers. He counted the seconds by heartbeats. "Do you want to look first?" he asked.

She shook her head.

He reached across her, picked it up. "Not pregnant."

Her body jerked, as if he'd struck her. She jumped out of bed and ran down the hall. He heard her slam her bedroom door shut.

Should he go to her? Let her be?

He looked at the results again, let it sink in. It was what he'd wanted, the best answer possible.

So, why did he feel so hollow?

He got up and dressed, walked down the hall. He started to knock on her door then could hear the shower running, so he went downstairs and restarted the fire. After a while, she came down, dressed for an evening at her brother's house, even wearing makeup, which she rarely did.

"Still don't want to come?" she asked.

"No."

He met her at the bottom of the staircase. "We dodged a bullet," he said, wishing he could feel the relief he should.

She met his gaze straight on. "Looks like it."

He knew there was more they should be saying, but it all felt too raw to him. Maybe tomorrow.

She turned away abruptly and headed to the kitchen. "There's chili in the fridge, if you want to reheat it. I'll see you later."

He saw her grab a plate covered with foil and then open the door to the garage. Soon her car was moving down the driveway. Rain was coming down in earnest. He hadn't even noticed it had started.

He'd thought his world would right itself again when

he knew whether she was pregnant or not. If she was, he would've had something to do—plan a quick wedding. If she wasn't, he could relax.

Instead, he felt a deep loss. He'd convinced himself she was pregnant, even with little reason to think so. Was he mourning for what had never existed?

He sank onto the sofa and dropped his head in his hands. He hadn't had anyone in his life who was just his, someone to put above all others. Someone to cherish, who would cherish him in return. This was the closest he'd come, and it had taken him years to allow it, to take a chance, to open up about his past. She hadn't been judgmental, but had shared her past, too.

At least about everything except why she'd run away in the first place. She continued to balk about that.

Where did this leave him now? And her? And Emma, who gave him kisses before bed now. They'd come a long way.

He didn't eat dinner. He barely even left the couch all evening. When she hadn't come home by eleven o'clock, he was frantic. The rain had barely let up all night. What if she'd had an accident driving home?

He'd just picked up his phone to call Gavin when he saw headlights coming up his driveway. Please don't be the sheriff…

It was Shana, safe and sound. He took a minute to catch his breath then he went through the kitchen into the garage. "Have fun?" he asked.

"Yes. Dylan came, too. We laughed a whole lot." Her tone held a bit of accusation in it, which he ignored. He couldn't have spent the evening trying to laugh.

"Any word on Joe and Dixie?"

"Gavin spoke to her this morning. They probably won't be here until closer to New Year's."

He opened the back door and got a sleeping Emma out of her car seat. She was deadweight in his arms. He carried her upstairs and settled her in her crib, but she didn't open her eyes for a second. He moved aside as Shana pulled up Emma's comforter and tucked it around her. She kissed her fingertips and pressed them to Emma's forehead then brushed back her hair.

Finally she looked at him. "Good night," she said, then she turned around and walked away, leaving him to go to his bed alone.

He'd been alone most of his adult life, but this was the loneliest he'd ever felt.

Shana was still awake at 2:00 a.m. She'd lied to Kincaid—she hadn't had fun at Gavin's. She'd tried, and she'd made herself laugh, but it had been one of the hardest evenings of her life. Becca was pregnant and due in April. Marcy was due in May. They were both jubilant in their pregnancies and they had loving, attentive husbands who were excited to be first-time fathers and had no qualms about showing it.

Shana felt wrung through the wringer. She knew it was best that she wasn't pregnant. Was sure of that. But she'd been hoping for more from Kincaid, that he would still want to marry her.

He'd seemed upset at the test results, but in what way? She'd thought that giving him the evening alone would let him come to terms with everything, but he didn't bring it up, so she'd decided to sleep alone.

Except she wasn't sleeping. She couldn't relax, couldn't find peace. She was grieving for a baby that never existed, she recognized that. She didn't want to grieve alone.

She'd been brave about so many things in her life—alone. She was sick of it.

Shana got out of bed and walked down the hall. She didn't knock. He rose up in the bed but didn't question her, just lifted the covers, inviting her to join him.

She got into bed, curved herself into him, spooning, feeling his body against hers all the way to her feet. His arm came around her stomach, and he tucked her a little closer, if that was possible.

"I was cold," she said.

"Me, too."

Then she closed her eyes and slept.

Chapter Thirteen

When the people of Chance City threw a party, they did it right, Shana thought. Somehow it had turned into an open house so that more people could attend, staggering arrivals and departures to accommodate everyone who wanted to come. Those who could give, gave. Those who couldn't, received graciously.

They'd changed the venue three times as they foresaw their attendance growing, finally ending up at the high school gymnasium, which also had a kitchen. Bruno Manning played Santa brilliantly, as it turned out, no padding necessary.

At the end of the evening, Shana held Emma and watched Doc and Aggie as they stood on stage, waiting for quiet. Although some of the guests had left, most remained. There was enough food left over to give boxes

to those who needed it, and many of the local businesses had donated gifts for the children.

She looked around for Kincaid. She'd barely seen
him all day. They had both been busy, had crossed
paths a few times, but that was all. She'd gotten up
before him this morning, leaving him sleeping, and they
hadn't had a minute alone since.

She finally spotted him talking to her father, of all
people. Deep in conversation, they didn't seem to notice
the crowd noise dwindling until Doc finally spoke, the
sound system squawking, making everyone cover their
ears and laugh.

"Merry Christmas, everyone!" Doc called out, re-
ceiving an en masse greeting in return. "Have you enjoyed yourselves?"

The response was deafening.

"Good, because your party committee held a quick
meeting a few minutes ago and decided that we'll be
calling this our first annual Share the Spirit party."

More hoots and hollers went up.

"I don't know why we waited this long," Doc said.
"Now, there are lots of people here that need thanking,
but to a one, everybody said they didn't want thanks.
That's the spirit of Christmas at work, folks. So, one
big thank-you to everyone who helped, everyone who
came and everyone who's going to stick around and
help clean up," he added, shaking a finger at them.

Laughter filled the room. No doubt the room would
be back to rights in record time with the help of many
willing hands.

"Just one last announcement," Doc said, a hitch in

his voice. He took Aggie's hand. A hum ran through the crowd. "This beautiful lady, Aggie McCoy, has agreed to become my wife, and I'm telling you, it's the best Christmas present I've ever had."

"Jeez, Mom!" came a loud voice from across the room. "We come home after six months, try to surprise you, and you steal our thunder!"

"Joe's home!" Aggie screamed, then gasped, "Oh, my word. Dixie's pregnant!"

Excited, Shana went up on tiptoe, but couldn't see her sister, so she pushed her way through the crowd, which had tightened as all the McCoys surrounded them.

"Move aside," Aggie said with authority, and people did.

Shana followed, letting Aggie clear the path. While Joe hugged Aggie, Dixie grabbed Shana and Emma together. They hugged for a long time—until Emma started to complain—then they moved apart. Shana fluffed her sister's hair, which had gotten long and even curlier. She put her hand on Dixie's belly.

"How far?" she asked.

"Four months. Looks like it's going to be babies galore, come spring." She pulled Shana back for another hug. "I've missed you so much. And look at my sweet niece Emma. How big you've grown."

"So big," Emma said.

Dixie laughed. "Yes. Are Mom and Dad— Gavin! Oh, is this Becca? I'm so glad to meet you finally."

The reunion went on, the congratulations endless to Aggie and Doc, to Dixie and Joe. Shana was overwhelmed by it all. She'd already been teetering on the edge of reason and control. Now she feared falling off. Dixie was pregnant, too. It was an epidemic.

She saw her parents hovering at the fringes of the crowd. Shana caught Dixie's attention and pointed. Dixie extricated herself and went to them. Her mother was beaming, even her father smiled.

It was too much for Shana. Dixie had the life Shana wanted—marriage, a child with the man she loved and visible love from her parents.

"Do you need to get out of here?" Kincaid asked from right beside her.

She nodded.

He lifted Emma out of her arms, took Shana by the elbow and guided her outdoors toward the parking lot.

"I don't need to go home," she said, realizing she really couldn't just disappear, not now. "I just need a minute to regroup."

"Let's walk a little ways."

"We don't have jackets." She looked around at everything, at nothing.

"It's hard for you to see your parents with Dixie, isn't it?"

Tears stung her eyes. "Terribly hard. I know she's the good daughter, the one who didn't run away or have a baby without being married. She stayed and helped them with the store for years, putting herself second. I was selfish."

"What happened to make you leave, Shana?"

She blew out a breath, knowing she couldn't hold it back any longer. "It wasn't one thing in particular, but years of feeling like a pariah. I didn't understand it, didn't know why they didn't treat me the same as Dixie. Of course, I wasn't her. I was me, and that was the answer."

"You butted heads?"

"Everything I did was wrong. Unlike Gavin and Dixie, I was socially inept. And Gavin got straight As without trying hard. They figured out how to keep the peace with Dad, or maybe they were just better at ignoring him. I argued. I would go without speaking to him for weeks, but he didn't seem to care. That smile that he had for Dixie tonight? I can't remember that directed at me."

"The story as I heard it was that you took off before your graduation ceremony and didn't tell anyone that you were going or where."

"That's right." As a parent now, she recognized how cruel that had been. But then? Then it was the only solution she could see. "You want to know the worst of it, Kincaid?"

"Yes."

The memory hurt as much today as it had that day, all those years ago. "A week before graduation, I got into a shouting match with my father, and he told me he couldn't wait for me to graduate and leave home. And my mother stood right next to him and didn't say a word. So I punished them. For ten years I stayed away, but who was I really punishing? I see it all differently now, with the perspective of time. I caused a lot of my own problems. I craved his attention, and he wasn't capable of giving it. Mom tried her best, but it was never enough for me."

"You said once that you just want him to forgive you. Maybe what you need is to take action yourself, to do something you *can* control now. You can forgive *him,* Shana. I can tell you from experience that it helps."

Emma started to fuss. "Brrr," she said, but she was probably also picking up on Shana's tension.

"We'll go inside right now, peapod." As they walked toward the building, Shana said, "Thank you. You gave me perspective that was missing."

"You've proven you *can* take care of yourself, you know. You've done great."

"With Dixie's help at first, and now yours, but I appreciate the support." She knew she sounded prim, but she had to keep her emotional distance from him. He was obviously still her friend, but not her future. She needed to stop leaning on him.

She probably needed to stop sleeping with him. But could she?

They ran into Gavin just inside the door. "Did you know they were coming home today?" Shana asked before he could question where she and Kincaid had been.

"I was sworn to secrecy. They wanted to surprise everyone."

"They did a good job of it."

"So did Doc and Aggie," Gavin said. "I can't believe they pulled that one off. They really surprised everyone."

"Not me," Shana said a little smugly, feeling both

men stare at her. "I've known for a while. They asked me to figure out a way to combine their households. I spent hours at both their houses coming up with a plan."

"How long ago did you find out?" Kincaid asked.

"Two weeks, and it wasn't always easy to keep my mouth shut. I'm so happy for them."

"We're taking the party to Joe and Dixie's after this. It won't be a late night," Gavin said, turning to leave. "Be there or be square. You're the star of the hour, Kincaid," he added. "We can't wait to see what you've done with the house. If it's anything close to what you did for Becca and me, they'll be thrilled."

The gymnasium was cleaned in record time with so many helping hands, then people left to spend Christmas Eve with their families. For the McCoys that meant a crowd squeezed into Joe and Dixie's newly remodeled house. It wasn't long before Emma said she wanted to go to bed, so Shana got out a portable crib and put Emma down.

As Shana was leaving the bedroom, she came across Dixie, waiting outside. Dixie swept her into a big hug and didn't let go for a long time. "Thank you for my beautiful home," she said.

"It's mostly Kincaid's doing."

"Your talented hand is everywhere, right down to the new lemon-yellow dish towels." They separated but still held hands. "I need to escape the noise for a few minutes. Want to come sit with me?"

"I'd love to," Shana said. "Poor Emma's on overload, too. Santa really confused her, then it was downhill for a quite a while after. She clung."

"I love how she calls me Dizzy."

"I showed her your picture every day." They ended up in the brand-new master bedroom, seated in two chairs in front of a fireplace. All they needed to do was flip a switch to start it.

"Such a lazy way to start a fire. Thank goodness," Dixie said, laying a hand on her slightly rounded belly. "It's been a very long twenty-four hours of traveling."

Shana watched her massage her abdomen. "Do you know what you're having?"

"We decided we'd wait and be surprised. It doesn't matter which sex it is. So, I want to hear about you. How's everything working out with Kincaid? You seem to be getting along."

Shana started to say that everything was fine, but the words that came out were, "Oh, Dixie. Everything is a mess. Nothing's working out the way it was supposed to."

It all spilled from her then, the pain and sorrow, the joy and excitement.

"I don't know what to do, Dix." She dabbed at her eyes with a tissue, blew her nose hard.

"I had more faith in him than that." Her voice and expression were cold.

"Faith? I don't understand. We both were attracted. We both acted on it."

"I…I talked to him right after you told me you were moving in with him. He promised me he would take care of you, but all he's done is hurt you."

"That's not true. I'm just as responsible."

"He made me a promise, Shana. He didn't keep it."

"Well, maybe he couldn't help it. Maybe what he felt for me overruled his promise to you." She said it coolly, not wanting anything negative said against the man she loved.

Dixie raised her brows. "Maybe it did."

"I'm sorry." Shana blew out a breath. "I shouldn't be taking this out on you. And my relationship with Kincaid will resolve itself somehow." She stood. "I've kept you long enough."

They went downstairs and found that almost everyone had left. Only Kincaid, Gavin and Becca were left.

"Are you okay?" Joe asked Dixie, coming up to her.

"I am exhausted." She zeroed in on Kincaid, but everyone hopped up and made their farewells, Shana going back upstairs to collect Emma, hoping Dixie wouldn't lay into Kincaid right then and there.

"It's gotten icy," he said as they left. "We can take my truck and come back tomorrow for your car."

"Emma's car seat," she said with a shake of her head.

"I bought one and installed it today in my truck."

"Why?"

"For times like this."

That suggested permanence to her....

She was too worn out to think about it. Shana didn't bother to change Emma into her sleepers, but undressed her down to a T-shirt and tights.

There didn't seem to be a question of where Shana would sleep tonight. Kincaid took her hand and walked her to his bedroom. They undressed and climbed into bed. He turned out the bedside lamp.

"You were crying," he said after they were wrapped up together. "At Dixie's."

"Happy tears." And there she went, telling another lie, but it was too late and she didn't have the energy for anything more. "I'm glad she's home."

He dragged a hand down her back and over her rear, pulling her leg over his, bringing her closer.

"I owe you an apology," he said, the words quiet yet seeming loud in the dark room.

"For?"

"I saw your car outside Doc's the day you must have been cataloguing his house. You were there a long time, and I jumped to some conclusions."

She pulled back to look at him. "What conclusions?"

"I questioned you about the errands you did, and you didn't mention seeing Doc, so I thought you were keeping something important from me. That you were seeing him as a patient. That maybe you'd gone to get the morning-after pill—or something."

"Technically, it was two mornings after." She studied his face. "You asked about Doc, and I told you. I just wasn't specific."

"You'd left him out at first, then you'd hesitated when I asked. I didn't trust you, Shana. I'm sorry for that."

"Is that why you've been so distant?"

"I was angry that you'd gone behind my back about something I thought concerned us. *Just us.*"

Since she'd done her share of not being open about everything, she could hardly fault him. She was grateful to know there was a reason for his increasing distance from her.

"I probably could've told you," she said carefully, knowing the discussion could easily become too serious, too important, maybe even life-changing. He hadn't trusted her. That was big to her. But all she said was, "I know you would've kept Doc and Aggie's news to yourself, but I needed to honor their trust in me, you know?"

"I do know. Sometimes we can't be completely honest because we've been asked to keep something private." Kincaid ran his fingers through her hair, enjoying how she made soft sounds of appreciation. It seemed the right time to tell her another truth he hadn't spoken aloud to her. "It's good that you weren't pregnant, Shana."

There was a long moment of silence, then she said, "Yes."

Which wasn't much of a response, he decided. "And it's good that your sister has come home." Although the look Dixie had given him at her house didn't bode well for his continued friendship with her. He had a feeling Shana had told Dixie everything—and Kincaid was going to hear about it.

"She's also my best friend," Shana said. "I'm beyond happy she's home."

She yawned, and he tucked her tightly against him and shut his eyes. He had spent the day figuring out what he needed to do about her, had even started the process.

The unknown factor was how she would feel about

it, but he'd always been willing to take chances. Usually they worked out, but sometimes they fizzled, even when he thought it was a sure thing.

And this was far from a sure thing.

Chapter Fourteen

Shana had spent so much time and energy trying to make Christmas special that when it finally came, it was a letdown. She'd built it up too much in her mind. She'd wanted to give her little girl a perfect day. She'd wanted to give Kincaid a Christmas worth remembering for once.

Instead, a pall hung over the day.

It's good that you weren't pregnant, he'd said last night. That would seem to be something that made him happy, yet he wasn't. Oh, he was doing a good job of pretending. He handed out gifts, looked anxious for her reaction to them, but something was missing. He wasn't relaxed. In fact, at times he seemed uncomfortable around her. Why? Everything was back to normal—wasn't it?

She didn't have an answer to that question, but even with all that going on, it was the best Christmas of Shana's memory. Emma was all decked out in a white sweater, red tutu skirt, white tights and red sneakers, all gifts from Kincaid, who'd surprised mother and daughter with a mound of presents that took so long to open, Emma lost interest.

Shana hadn't. Every box she unwrapped communicated something from him—the fact he paid attention whenever she'd wished out loud for a particular something, like a full-size mixer instead of the hand mixer, and a warmer, longer raincoat. He'd bought a stack of romantic comedy DVDs because that was what she always rented. And he presented her with her own rechargeable drill. What woman wouldn't love a man who listened that well?

"What are you smiling about?" he asked as he shoved used wrapping paper into a bag.

"You."

He raised his brows.

"Best Christmas ever, Kincaid."

He nodded, looking way too serious. "Same here."

She'd had a little trouble finding gifts for the man who had everything, but she'd finally been successful, starting with filling a stocking for him as well as Emma, his containing silly items like gum and oranges and a deck of cards, even batteries. He said he'd never had a stocking before, and the pleasure of watching him unwrap every item was her best gift. She'd found a sweater the same color blue as his eyes, and a new down vest for away from construction sites, where his old, well-used vest was still fine.

But the most fun she had was making a photo book of all his construction projects. She'd secretly worked at his computer, using before and after shots he'd taken to create a book she'd had printed online and shipped to her. It was something he could show clients, but also could just sit and look at and feel pride in what he'd done.

She could tell he loved it, and was totally surprised by her gift. She figured she could do a new one every few years....

"Kinky!"

"What, Miss Emma?"

"Come. Play."

"Please," Shana reminded her.

"Peese."

While they stacked blocks, Shana made pancakes, using her new griddle. When Kincaid brought Emma into the kitchen, he put her in her high chair and found a large bib to cover her pretty Christmas sweater.

How quickly they'd all become a family. How would it affect Emma if it changed?

"Mmm," Emma said as Shana put her plate in front of her. "Cake."

"Pancakes, yes. And apples."

"Mmm." Kincaid did a perfect imitation as Shana set down their plates, making her smile. "What's the plan for the day?" he asked.

"Well, there's Aggie's open house. I'd like to do that."

"Okay."

"And I've decided to go see my parents."

He studied her but didn't say anything for a few seconds. "Gavin and Becca are hosting Christmas dinner. You'll see them there."

"I have cookies to take them. Mom has always loved the holiday, so I'm thinking I'll catch her in a good mood. Maybe Dad, too. I want just a minute with them, without the rest of the family."

"Would you like me to go with you?"

"Thank you for the offer, but it should just be Emma and me. We could stop in on our way to Aggie's."

"Done."

Shana packaged the cookies to take to her parents and also some for Aggie. When she was done, she decided to put Emma down for a morning nap. She went in search of her and Kincaid. She hadn't heard them for a while, so she figured they were in Emma's room. But as Shana passed through the living room she saw them on the couch, Kincaid stretched out, asleep, with Emma in dreamland on his chest.

Swallowing hard, Shana moved closer, not wanting to disturb them. She took a picture in her mind and framed it there forever.

Will you marry me? she asked silently. She curled up in his chair to watch them, was still watching when he woke up a half hour later.

He saw her sitting there. "She's heavier than she seems," he said quietly.

Shana smiled. "You two have come a long way in a month."

"So have we."

"True." And yet not far enough. "I need to go gird my loins," she said, standing.

"You don't have to do this today, Shana."

"I want to." She came closer to him. "Shall I take her?"

"She's fine."

It would've been the easiest thing in the world to just walk over and give each of them a kiss before she went upstairs. She didn't know how much longer she could hold back everything she felt inside.

An hour later they were on the road. They pulled up in front of her parents' house.

She got out of the truck and opened the back door to grab her box of cookies as Kincaid got Emma from her car seat.

"We won't be long," Shana said to him.

"I'll be right here."

She nodded. It was nice having a partner.

She went to the front door and knocked. Her mother opened it. "Shana. Why— Malcolm. Shana's here."

"Merry Christmas, Mom."

"Come in. Hello, Emma."

Emma smiled shyly, her finger in her mouth.

"Some cookies for you and Dad," Shana said, handing her mother the decorated box. The living room was cozy, the fireplace lit. A tree was up and decorated, a few gifts under it.

"Have you talked to Dixie or Gavin today?" her mother asked.

"I talked to Gavin, but Dixie was still asleep, Joe said. How are you, Dad? Merry Christmas."

"Same to you."

"We have a gift for Emma," her mother said. "I'd planned to take it to Gavin's."

"That's fine. She can wait. It'll be fun for her."

Silence descended. They all stood in the middle of the room, not looking at each other, but not as uncomfortable as other times. "Well, I guess we should be going."

"I suppose you're headed to Aggie's," her mother said.

"For a little while, yes. Are you going?" The invitation was open—the more, the merrier, Aggie always said.

"We thought we'd just stay home by the fire until we go to Gavin's."

"It's always fun, Mom. There'll be lots of people you know." She headed toward the door. "It's really casual. You wouldn't have to stay long."

"It's not something I care to do," her mother said.

"Okay." She put her hand on the doorknob. "We'll see you—"

"Why can't you see how much you hurt your mother by always being with Aggie?" her father said.

Shana was so startled at the number of words he'd said, she almost didn't comprehend them. "What? Wait, what are you talking about?"

"Malcolm, please."

"Hush, Bea. This needs saying."

"Not on Christmas."

"Why not? We've been silent long enough."

Dread rooted Shana in place. "Go ahead. Tell me." If it cleared the air so that they could get beyond their past, she was all for it.

"Ever since you came home," her father said, "you've treated Aggie more like your mother than your own. It's hurtful. I know it was easier for you because there's no history there. It's all fun and games with Aggie. Everyone loves Aggie the perfect."

That anyone should slam Aggie, who'd been her savior this past year, was beyond Shana's comprehension. She kept her voice as level as possible, but she was angry. "Aggie opened her arms to me. You shut your door in my face. I wanted to reach out, to repair our relationship. I know I made mistakes, big ones, but I've finally learned to forgive myself for them."

And she had, she realized. Thanks to Kincaid.

She walked back to her mother. "I love you, Mom." She kissed her cheek and gave her a hug, Emma squirming in her arms. Then she went to her father. "I love you, Dad." He stood with his hands loosely at his sides, but he allowed the hug.

She went to the door, adding, "My heart is open to you, but you have to reach out, too. Merry Christmas."

I forgive you. She didn't say the words out loud, but it was enough.

"Wait, Shana. Please wait," her mother said. She glanced at her husband. "I'd like to be closer," her mother said, her voice quaking. "I'd like us to be like... other families. Please, Malcolm. We're not getting any younger."

After a few long, harrowing seconds, he nodded.

The burning coals in Shana's stomach cooled a little. She unclenched her fists. "We'll see you at Gavin's," she said, then she left, sensing they needed a little time and space right now. She did, too. It was a lot to take in at once.

She passed Emma to Kincaid, then managed to get herself into the car, weak knees and all. "Just drive. Please."

"Was it that bad?" Kincaid asked after a minute.

"No." Tears pushed at her eyes. "Actually, there's hope."

He reached across to squeeze her hand. She squeezed back. "I forgave myself for all I did to cause them pain," she whispered. "And I forgave them, too."

"Good."

"I'm moving on. Moving forward." She felt stronger now, as if she could do anything. "Thank you," she said. "You were right."

They drove to Aggie's. So far, only a small mob had gathered, but it was also a daylong event. People would come and go. Kincaid had never gone before, even though he'd been invited forever. Everyone greeted him like an old friend. He wasn't even anxious to escape.

He watched Shana move through the crowd, saw Dylan talking with two kids his age. Dylan waved at Kincaid, then pointed to his feet to show he was wearing the new boots Kincaid had given him for Christmas. The boy had found a home here, a community of his own.

Kincaid went out to the backyard and joined the men

standing around the tall propane heaters. Doc, Aggie's sons Jake and Donovan, and a couple of sons-in-law were watching the kids play in the yard and on the swings. Kincaid greeted everyone, felt their welcome in return. Felt that he fit in.

The talk was of football, a subject near and dear to his heart. A few of the women wandered out, including Shana, who took Emma to a swing and settled her in it. Shana seemed more relaxed, but that could be because she was at Aggie's. No one could be tense in her house.

"That little Emma's a cutie," said the man standing next to Kincaid. He was one of Aggie's five sons-in-law, and Kincaid's accountant.

"And a whirlwind. But then, you know what that's like, Steve. You've got a few of your own."

"All grown up now. No longer tax deductions. I miss those days." He sighed dramatically. "Maybe Emma will be your tax deduction by next year."

The statement didn't go unnoticed, although he could tell Shana was pretending not to have heard it.

"Which reminds me," Steve said. "Is there a reason why you haven't turned in any of your December receipts? You're usually on top of these things. Cher and I decided to get away for a couple of weeks before tax season hits in full force, and I know you like to file as early as possible. Everything else is done. It won't take much time at all."

Kincaid's gaze connected with Shana's. Had she understood what Steve meant? Did she realize Kincaid had given her busywork when he'd asked her to enter his "unorganized mess" into a spreadsheet? He couldn't tell from her expression if she got it or not, because she turned her back on him and focused on Emma.

The pleasure of the day seeped out. For all that they'd talked about the importance of honesty, they'd told lies or kept secrets. Maybe he should just tell her the truth about why he'd hired her, get it out there, let them deal with it rather than having it hanging over his head.

He'd disappointed Dixie, too, and now she was angry at him. Then there was Aggie, who'd made the call to Dixie.

Yeah, he needed to talk to Dixie and figure out how to handle the situation. Shana deserved the truth— and a clean slate. If they had to start over, they would. She had already become important to his business, had proven herself competent in many ways. He didn't regret hiring her.

He did regret how he'd handled everything else.

Shana came up to him then, carrying Emma. "We're going to walk to Dixie's and pick up my car."

"You're ready to leave?"

"Yes." Her voice was cold as ice.

"I'll drive you."

"It's a few blocks. The walk will do me good. Clear my head, you know?" She said a marginally cheerful goodbye to everyone then disappeared into the house.

Should he follow her? Catch up? Explain? It should be a private discussion, not one open to the citizens of Chance City. Should he just go home and wait for her? Try to talk to her at Joe and Dixie's?

He was in a quandary like never before. He could

stumble no matter what he did, because she was unpredictable, something he usually liked about her.

In the end, he hung around for about fifteen minutes then headed home to wait, feeling like a dead man walking.

Chapter Fifteen

"You need to come clean with me right now," Shana said to her sister as they sat in her living room. "Because you know a whole lot more than you've let on. Spill."

Joe was gone, having been banished to Aggie's house and taking Emma with him.

"I'll tell you what I know—and take the heat for it—but I want you to understand that we acted in good faith, Shana. We wanted your life to be not as much of a struggle. Please keep that in mind."

"This oughta be good." Shana crossed her arms. She tried to stop her foot from bouncing but couldn't. So much anger was pent up inside her, it was her only outlet.

"Aggie called me—"

"Aggie? She's part of this plot, too?" Shana couldn't believe it. Aggie said she hadn't told anyone. No, that's wasn't right. She'd said she hadn't told *Kincaid*. That sneaky woman. "Are there any others?"

"No. Just Aggie, Kincaid and me. Well, Joe knows, but none of us has told anyone. Unless Aggie told Doc, which could have happen—"

"In other words, the whole town could know."

"No. Don't think that. At the most, it's the people I just named, and you know we'll all keep it confidential."

"I don't know that at all."

"Knock it off, would you? You know darn well that none of us would talk about this to anyone else. Do you want the story or not?"

I would've rather heard it from Kincaid, she thought, beyond disappointed in him. She felt duped. How much was a lie? How could she have fallen in love with such a deceitful man? "I'm all ears."

"I'm telling you this because I know Kincaid would feel an obligation not to break my confidence, which leaves him in a big bind. So, this will free him of the promise he made me. Which he only half kept, as it turns out, but the other half is up to him to fix. I never foresaw you sleeping with him."

Dixie looked away for a minute, as if trying to find where she left off. "Okay. So. Aggie called me after you had some kind of breakdown on Thanksgiving. She was scared for you, Shana. And she did the right thing by letting me know. I knew you wouldn't accept financial help from me or Gavin, or anyone. Kincaid was the only person I thought of who might be able to find a better job situation for you, because he gets around a lot for his business. I left it in his competent hands. I didn't know how he would make it happen, but he got more creative than I anticipated. Suddenly you were living with him."

"He evicted me."

"To give you a better life for you and Emma."

"Don't sugarcoat it, Dixie. He did this for you, not for me or Emma. And he's kept his businesses booming all these years without my help. He will continue for many more. I'm a figurehead. A gofer. A toolbox-wielding lackey. A shill. A—"

"I get it. Really, Shana, you know he wouldn't pay you to be doing nothing of value."

"Oh, well, I guess he does seem to like the way I wash his underwear. Briefs, by the way." Her foot bounced a little higher. She couldn't control it at all.

Dixie laughed. "Good to know." She put up both hands. "I know. I'm sorry. It isn't funny. Look, I'm pretty sure you wouldn't have slept with him unless you cared about him a lot. He's an honorable man, so I figure he couldn't help himself, either. And when you get right down to it, you actually seemed a little disappointed that you weren't pregnant."

Shana shoved herself off the sofa and stalked to the front window. A couple of kids were riding bikes, probably Christmas presents. The everyday activity calmed her. Life went on.

"Maybe I was. A little," she said. "I didn't know it until I wasn't. Then it hit hard."

"I get that." Dixie joined her at the window. She wrapped her arm around Shana's shoulders. "When I took my first pregnancy test, it was negative. So, I know how that feels. Then when my period still didn't come, I tried it again. Bingo."

Shana went silent as she thought that through. "I hadn't considered that I might have to test again. I waited a full two weeks."

"Did you test first thing in the morning?"

"No. No, late in the day." Because they'd reached a point where he'd needed to know. She'd read all the instructions. She should've waited.

"The hormones can be diluted by then. False negative. You should probably try once more, but wait until morning."

"What if I am, Dix?"

"You and Kincaid will figure it out."

He'll make me marry him. He'd said they'd dodged a bullet. He didn't want to marry her at all. "I'm just starting to connect with Mom and Dad again."

"It's still early. They don't have to know when you got pregnant. And as long as you're married, they probably won't care."

"Kincaid and I have a lot to figure out before that can happen, Dix."

"You will."

Shana sighed. "I can't do another test in the morning because I have to pick one up first, and it's Christmas. And I have to drive to Grass Valley, like I did before, so no one in town sees what I'm buying."

"So, that's what you'll do. Do you have to work to-morrow?"

She shook her head. "We're taking a break until after New Year's." Which meant they'd both be hanging around the house all week. "I could help you get the nursery together this week."

Dixie gave her an all-knowing smile. "We'll see. For now, go talk to Kincaid. Clear the air."

The drive back to Aggie's was almost painful. She didn't want to talk to him, but she had to talk to him. She barely saw the road, could hardly catch her breath. Then she got to Aggie's and learned he'd left. She gathered up Emma and headed home—well, to Kincaid's house. His truck was out front. She didn't know if she was relieved or not.

Until today, she thought she'd finally found a place where she could feel good and safe—and happy. She'd been hopeful, and look where that always got her. She was beyond tears, her devastation was so deep.

"Home," Emma said from the backseat.

"Maybe," Shana whispered. She pulled into the garage with the same dread she'd had before she'd walked up to her parents' front door.

And the same hope.

When would she ever learn?

Kincaid heard the garage door opening. He'd been sitting in his chair, staring at the tree, waiting. Just waiting. Dixie had called to say she'd released him of his promise to her, that she'd told Shana she'd asked for his help. Of course, he'd given more help than she'd asked for. And now he was paying for it.

He scrubbed his face with his hands then stood. He wasn't a coward. He would meet her in the garage as he always did, take Emma from her car seat and carry her inside.

She gave him a steady look but opened the back door herself. He shoved his hands in his pockets, feeling at a loss, then Emma called out, "Kinky!" Meaning, "I want Kinky to get me out," he figured.

Shana stepped away to let him. Emma patted his face with both hands as he unbuckled her. "My Kinky," she said, but this time in a voice that sounded like someone saying, "Good boy," to the family dog. It made him smile.

"She needs a nap," Shana said as they got inside the house.

"Night night," Emma said.

So they all went upstairs, but then Shana said, "I'll take it from here."

And so it begins, he thought. She'd already made up her mind about what she wanted to do. But was she just distancing herself and her daughter emotionally or was she going to make a physical change, cut him out completely?

In the living room he stoked the fire, added a new log. When she finally came downstairs, she look composed.

"I know this may sound convenient," he said, "but I'd already decided to ask Dixie to let me tell you the truth."

"Because you got caught in a lie or because it was the right thing to do?" She took a seat, folded her hands in her lap. "I thought I finally wouldn't be anybody's charity case, thanks to you. You totally had me convinced you were hiring me for my *skills*. You said you *needed* me. But actually I became *your* charity case."

She seemed eerily calm, so he couldn't figure out where he stood. "Maybe I didn't originally hire you for your skills, but it became evident almost immediately how multitalented you are. And competent. And creative. You've become invaluable, and that's the truth."

"Were you attracted to me, you know, physically?"

"When I hired you? Yes," he said then added quickly when she frowned, "but I didn't know it. I swear to you, I did not hire you expecting to sleep with you. You just became…irresistible."

If he could just get her to stay another week, he thought, then all would be well. Even just a few more days. If she left, he might not ever get her back. He needed the proximity. "Please don't leave, Shana."

She made a sound of frustration, then stood and went to the front window. "I don't— Oh, no. My mom just pulled up. Great timing, Mom."

Kincaid went to the front door when Shana seemed frozen in place. "Merry Christmas, Bea."

"The same to you, Kincaid. Your tree is beautiful."

"Thank you. Did you want to be alone with Shana?"

"No, it's fine." She went to where Shana stood and handed her an envelope. "Your baby pictures, as promised. There's one of you at eighteen months that looks just like Emma."

Shana clutched the envelope to her chest. "Thanks, Mom. I appreciate it." Her voice shook.

"I'm sorry your father didn't come with me, but I truly think everything will work out. He's seeing the years pass so fast, just like I am. What you said to him today opened his eyes." She ran a hand down Shana's hair. "We want to be real grandparents. Maybe we won't be as intense about it as Aggie, but it'll be better than it was. And honey, I forgive you."

Shana hugged her, a small sob escaping. Kincaid could only watch in silence and hope her father did the same so that she wasn't disappointed or hurt again.

"I'll leave you to your afternoon," Bea said. Then she was gone.

Shana opened the envelope and found the picture Bea spoke of. She showed it to Kincaid. "I've always said she looks just like you," he said. "Obviously going to see them this morning turned out to be the right thing to do."

"Christmas miracles," she said. She looked at him. "You asked me not to leave. Where would I go? You took away my apartment. I'm sure either Gavin or Dixie would take me in, but that would give the town something new to talk about. I'm making headway with my parents. I don't want to disrupt that."

He relaxed. He had time, the time he needed.

"But," she went on. "If the situation here goes downhill or gets too tense, I'll need to go. We need to try to go back to the beginning. As in, I'll be sleeping in my own room."

He was okay with that—for now. He'd been given what he wanted, the chance to start over with her.

"I'm sorry I wasn't honest with you."

"I understand that Dixie held you to a promise. But you all need to understand that I'm an adult with a child. I have to make my own decisions." She touched his arm, and it was like being touched by lightning. "I appreciate the job. I do. I want to keep on doing it. I just don't know if I can live with you."

"Baby steps, Shana."

For a second he thought she was going to kiss him, then she moved back a little.

"Gavin and Becca are hosting Christmas dinner," she said. "I plan to go. I'd like you to come, too, but if you don't want to, it's okay."

"I wouldn't want to be anywhere else."

"Okay." She sighed. "I'm going to catch a nap while I can."

"I'll be here."

He waited until she'd gotten upstairs before he let his legs buckle and he landed on the couch. He had a second chance.

This time he wouldn't blow it.

Chapter Sixteen

Pregnant.

Shana blinked and looked again at the results on the test stick. The word *Not* didn't magically appear. She lowered the stick to the bathroom counter, and then herself to the floor. Kincaid's words shouted in her head—*"We dodged a bullet."*

Well, the bullet had hit a bullseye, a teeny, tiny, nearly-impossible-to-hit bullseye.

It was 4:00 a.m. She'd been awake most of the night, waiting, finally giving up and taking the test. Before, when the results had been "Not Pregnant," she'd felt an unanticipated grief. Now she waited for joy to engulf her that she was.

What she felt was an urge to run far away, not to have to tell anyone, but especially Kincaid. "It's good that you weren't pregnant," he'd told her. He'd gone about these past few days believing that was true, and he'd been happy. Now she had to tell him otherwise.

And her family.

Shana leaned her head against the wall and stared at the ceiling. As much as she wanted to run, she'd spent the past year proving she wasn't that angry, scared girl anymore, just a human being, capable of making mistakes like everyone else.

Yesterday she'd tried to avoid Kincaid, but he hadn't let her. She'd driven to Grass Valley to buy another pregnancy test while he'd gone to Sacramento to do some house repairs for Marcy and Eric. When he got home mid-afternoon he had sought her out, then had barely left her side, maintaining an annoyingly upbeat mood, smiling so much she barely recognized him.

He and Emma had played a lot, too. He'd talked to her about going sledding in the snow in a couple of days. Emma had gotten so excited about it, even though she didn't know what it meant.

He'd been relaxed. She'd been so tense she almost felt herself breaking into pieces. She didn't want to bring him down from his happiness. And she really, really didn't want him to just do the right thing by her. She wanted him to love her.

But that was out of her control.

What she needed was a plan. She couldn't delay telling him, but she also didn't want to just have him come down to breakfast and get hit with the news. There must be a way of easing into it.

Maybe someone could take Emma for a couple of

hours so they wouldn't be interrupted. Shana could fix his favorite spaghetti and meatballs, get him all full and mellow, then she could say, "You know that pregnancy test I took the other day? Well, a funny thing happened…"

Funny. Right, it was hilarious.

He'd wanted to start over, to go back to the beginning, as employer and employee. *Sorry, Kincaid. No such luck.*

Shana's rear went to sleep as she sat there. She struggled to stand, then got into the shower, letting the hot water soothe her, rehearsing how she would tell him. Nothing seemed right.

When she was dressed she went downstairs and found him sitting on the couch, the tree lights on. Dawn hadn't broken yet. He wore flannel pajama bottoms and a T-shirt and was barefoot. She wondered if his feet were cold.

"Have you been there all night?" she asked, coming up beside him.

"No." He looked up at her and smiled. She was having difficulty getting used to a super-cheerful Kincaid. "You're up early, too," he said.

"One of those days, I guess." She sat at the end of the sofa.

"I've been thinking," he said.

"Uh-oh."

"I know. Dangerous, huh? We need a plan."

Hadn't she just thought that? "For what?"

"Work. Living together. Now that everything's out in the open, we should take some time to decide how we're going to manage our business and home lives so that everyone is comfortable."

"I thought you didn't like rules."

He flashed a grin. "They wouldn't be rules, but more like guidelines."

"Ah, I see. They're guidelines when you make them, but rules when I do."

"Pretty much, yes."

His cheerful mood had carried over from the day before. It was hard not to get caught up in it, except that she knew she would be ruining it later. "So, what are these guidelines?"

"I thought we could go somewhere for dinner tonight and work on them, just us, away from town and distractions. Somewhere neutral."

She could feel herself frowning. "Neutral? Why? If we stay here, do you think I'll start a fight?"

"Not necessarily."

Not necessarily? What did that mean? What kind of rules was he going to impose that he wanted her to be in public where she wouldn't make a scene? And she didn't want to tell him *her* news in public, which meant she would have to wait until after dinner, stretching out the agony.

Which actually wasn't such a horrible thought, she decided. She wasn't in a hurry to share her news. A nice dinner first, a little reprieve, couldn't hurt. "All right," she said. "I guess I should get a sitter."

"Mama!" Emma called.

"Looks like everyone's an early bird today," Shana said, getting up. She stopped next to him. "Thanks for trying to make things easier for us, Kincaid. I really appreciate it."

He gave her a quirky smile so unlike him she could only stare. "Good employer/employee relations are critical to successful job performance, I think," he said.

Boy, was he in for a surprise.

"Mama!"

"Hold your horses, Emma. I'm coming."

Emma neighed like a horse, something Kincaid had taught her yesterday.

It was a good start to what she imagined would be a very long day of anticipation.

And trepidation.

Kincaid had chosen a restaurant in Grass Valley that he'd never been to before, where there were no memories of any kind. He hoped the food was good, but it didn't matter at this point. He didn't think he would taste anything.

Shana looked beautiful. Beyond beautiful. Her cheeks were flushed, her eyes seemed a deeper green than ever. She'd even curled her hair in a really sexy way. And her dress? He could barely keep his eyes off the low neckline, under which she must be wearing a push-up bra, because she had more cleavage than he could recall.

It wasn't exactly how someone usually dressed for a business meeting.

But then, only he knew it wasn't a business meeting.

"Did you bring a list or something?" she asked as their salads plates were removed and their entrees set in front of them, chicken for her and steak for him.

"A list?"

"Your plan?"

"Oh." He tapped a finger to his temple. "It's all right here."

"Are you waiting for Bill Gates to join us or something before you start?"

He laughed. He knew she was nervous. Few people relished change, and he'd kept her guessing all day. "Okay. Well, now that you know I have an accountant, I'll be taking that job away from you."

"It was my least favorite task, anyway."

"What *is* your favorite?"

"Designing Mr. Broadburn's new bathroom is up there. I hope I get to do a lot more of that. But I've liked everything so far."

"And you're okay with everything you do at home?"

She nodded as she took a bite. "I get to spend a lot more time with Emma. I love that."

"Is there something you'd like to do that you're not doing?"

Her eyes lit up. "I'd like to decorate your downtown office. It's too sparse."

"People don't expect fancy from a contractor."

"Maybe not, but some large photos on the walls of some of your projects would give you something to show off. It looks cold, you know? It wouldn't cost much to fix it up."

As the meal went on, his nerves took over. Apparently so had hers, because neither of them ate more than half their dinner.

"May I interest you in dessert?" their server asked.

"I'm good, thanks," Shana said.

What? She always ate dessert. He'd counted on her eating dessert. "We can split something," he said.

She frowned. "You didn't even finish your dinner."

"Doesn't mean I don't want dessert. How about some chocolate mousse?" She loved chocolate.

"No, really, Kincaid. I'm full." She pressed a hand against her stomach as if emphasizing it.

"Bring us one, please," he said to the server, who gave a little bow.

Kincaid took a measured breath. The plan had been set in motion. "I bought the hardware store," he said.

"I'm pregnant," she said at the same time. "Wait, what?"

"What?" he asked, sitting back. "You're pregnant?"

She looked around. "Please. Everyone's looking."

"I live in Chance City. I'm used to it. Rewind, please." He gave a signal to the waiter to hold off, then he reached across the table and took her hand.

Her eyes welled. "I'm sorry," she said. "I did the test wrong. I'm pregnant."

Everything he had wished for, had come to hope for, lit up like neon in his head.

"I know you were glad I wasn't pregnant, but I kind of was not." Her voice shook. Her body shook. She looked scared.

"Shana, sweetheart. This is not bad news to me."

"It isn't?"

He pulled his chair closer to hers so that he could put his arm around her. "When we didn't know if you were pregnant, then found out you weren't, I realized how much I'd wanted it to be true."

"Why? Everyone will know we slept together right after I moved in."

"It doesn't matter to me. But you do. And Emma." He slid a hand over her abdomen. "And this one. I love you."

She threw her arms around him. "I love you, too. With all my heart."

"Your stubborn heart?" he asked tenderly.

She laughed a little shakily. "It wasn't so stubborn. In fact, it gave in pretty fast."

"Good, because I want a full-time commitment from you." He made a small gesture to their server, who brought a covered dish to the table then left. Kincaid lifted the lid, was surprised at how much his hands shook. Inside was a black velvet box. He opened it. "Shana Callahan, I want to share my life with you, now and forever. Will you marry me?"

"You had this all planned?"

"I set everything in motion Christmas Eve. I had to wait to get the ring yesterday. Well. Will you?"

"Yes! Oh, yes, of course."

He slipped the ring on her finger.

"It's stunning," she said holding up her hand to admire the diamond and emerald ring. "It's perfect."

"It matches your eyes."

She kissed him then while everyone around them applauded.

He tasted tears and knew they were happy ones. He was beyond happy himself. He would have a family of his own. He'd found the one success that had eluded him, the one he wanted most.

"What did you say about the hardware store?" she asked.

"I bought it."

She smiled in bemusement. "When?"

"Your father and I struck a deal at the Christmas Eve party."

"Why did you do that?"

"I'm looking at it as your bride price."

"Is that like a dowry? Aren't my parents supposed to pay *you* to take me off their hands?"

"In some cultures, a bride price is a symbol of the groom's estimation of his bride."

"And I'm only worth the price of a hardware store?" she said, acting affronted.

"I had a plan. I thought your parents would start traveling, and you would be happier, but then things changed on Christmas, so maybe that doesn't matter to you."

"It matters because they can retire and enjoy the rest of their lives. Unless you think you're going to get me to run the place."

He laughed, feeling better than he'd felt in his whole life. "What? You don't want to?"

She shook her head. "All I want is you."

"As someone said to me not long ago, take me, I'm yours."

* * * * *

HEART & HOME

Heartwarming romances where love can
happen right when you least expect it.

Harlequin
SPECIAL EDITION

COMING NEXT MONTH
AVAILABLE DECEMBER 27, 2011

#2161 FORTUNE'S CINDERELLA
The Fortunes of Texas: Whirlwind Romance
Karen Templeton

#2162 MOMMY IN THE MAKING
Northbridge Nuptials
Victoria Pade

#2163 DOCTORS IN THE WEDDING
Doctors in the Family
Gina Wilkins

#2164 THE DADDY DANCE
Mindy Klasky

#2165 THE HUSBAND RECIPE
Linda Winstead Jones

#2166 MADE FOR MARRIAGE
Helen Lacey

HSECNM1211

REQUEST YOUR FREE BOOKS!

2 FREE NOVELS PLUS 2 FREE GIFTS!

✦ Harlequin®

SPECIAL EDITION

Life, Love & Family

YES! Please send me 2 FREE Harlequin® Special Edition novels and my 2 FREE gifts (gifts are worth about $10). After receiving them, if I don't wish to receive any more books, I can return the shipping statement marked "cancel." If I don't cancel, I will receive 6 brand-new novels every month and be billed just $4.49 per book in the U.S. or $5.24 per book in Canada. That's a saving of at least 14% off the cover price! It's quite a bargain! Shipping and handling is just 50¢ per book in the U.S. and 75¢ per book in Canada.* I understand that accepting the 2 free books and gifts places me under no obligation to buy anything. I can always return a shipment and cancel at any time. Even if I never buy another book, the two free books and gifts are mine to keep forever.

235/335 HDN FEGF

Name	(PLEASE PRINT)

Address	Apt. #

City	State/Prov.	Zip/Postal Code

Signature (if under 18, a parent or guardian must sign)

Mail to the **Reader Service:**
IN U.S.A.: P.O. Box 1867, Buffalo, NY 14240-1867
IN CANADA: P.O. Box 609, Fort Erie, Ontario L2A 5X3

Not valid for current subscribers to Harlequin Special Edition books.

Want to try two free books from another line?
Call 1-800-873-8635 or visit www.ReaderService.com.

* Terms and prices subject to change without notice. Prices do not include applicable taxes. Sales tax applicable in N.Y. Canadian residents will be charged applicable taxes. Offer not valid in Quebec. This offer is limited to one order per household. All orders subject to credit approval. Credit or debit balances in a customer's account(s) may be offset by any other outstanding balance owed by or to the customer. Please allow 4 to 6 weeks for delivery. Offer available while quantities last.

Your Privacy—The Reader Service is committed to protecting your privacy. Our Privacy Policy is available online at www.ReaderService.com or upon request from the Reader Service.

We make a portion of our mailing list available to reputable third parties that offer products we believe may interest you. If you prefer that we not exchange your name with third parties, or if you wish to clarify or modify your communication preferences, please visit us at www.ReaderService.com/consumerschoice or write to us at Reader Service Preference Service, P.O. Box 9062, Buffalo, NY 14269. Include your complete name and address.

HSE11B

SPECIAL EDITION

Life, Love and Family

Karen Templeton

introduces

The FORTUNES *of* TEXAS: Whirlwind Romance

When a tornado destroys Red Rock, Texas, Christina Hastings finds herself trapped in the rubble with telecommunications heir Scott Fortune. He's handsome, smart and everything Christina has learned to guard herself against. As they await rescue, an unlikely attraction forms between the two and Scott soon finds himself wanting to know about this mysterious beauty. But can he catch Christina before she runs away from her true feelings?

FORTUNE'S CINDERELLA

Available December 27th wherever books are sold!

*Brittany Grayson survived a horrible ordeal at the hands
of a serial killer known as The Professional...
who's after her now?*

*Harlequin® Romantic Suspense presents a new installment
in Carla Cassidy's reader-favorite miniseries,*
LAWMEN OF BLACK ROCK.

*Enjoy a sneak peek of
TOOL BELT DEFENDER.*

*Available January 2012
from Harlequin® Romantic Suspense.*

"**B**rittany?" His voice was deep and pleasant and made
her realize she'd been staring at him openmouthed through
the screen door.

"Yes, I'm Brittany and you must be..." Her mind suddenly went blank.

"Alex. Alex Crawford, Chad's friend. You called him
about a deck?"

As she unlocked the screen, she realized she wasn't
quite ready yet to allow a stranger inside, especially a male
stranger.

"Yes, I did. It's nice to meet you, Alex. Let's walk around
back and I'll show you what I have in mind," she said. She
frowned as she realized there was no car in her driveway.
"Did you walk here?" she asked.

His eyes were a warm blue that stood out against his
tanned face and was complemented by his slightly shaggy
dark hair. "I live three doors up." He pointed up the street to
the Walker home that had been on the market for a while.

"How long have you lived there?"

"I moved in about six weeks ago," he replied as they

walked around the side of the house.

That explained why she didn't know the Walkers had moved out and Mr. Hard Body had moved in. Six weeks ago she'd still been living at her brother Benjamin's house trying to heal from the trauma she'd lived through.

As they reached the backyard she motioned toward the broken brick patio just outside the back door. "What I'd like is a wooden deck big enough to hold a barbecue pit and an umbrella table and, of course, lots of people."

He nodded and pulled a tape measure from his tool belt. "An outdoor entertainment area," he said.

"Exactly," she replied and watched as he began to walk the site. The last thing Brittany had wanted to think about over the past eight months of her life was men. But looking at Alex Crawford definitely gave her a slight flutter of pure feminine pleasure.

*Will Brittany be able to heal in the arms of Alex,
her hotter-than-sin handyman…or will a second
psychopath silence her forever? Find out in*
TOOL BELT DEFENDER
*Available January 2012
from Harlequin® Romantic Suspense
wherever books are sold.*

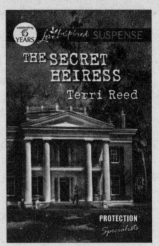